CODY F

MMONSTE

MICHAEL BRAY

CHAPTER ONE

Hebgen Lake,
Montana
August 17th, 1959

BILL SIMMS LOOKED OUT over the crystal clear waters of the lake and took in a very deliberate lungful of air, letting it out slowly for the benefit of his companion, a thin, sour-looking man called John Rogers. He patted a stubborn lock of his slick, waxed hair back into place and looked over the mountain ridge which was framed beautifully against the pastel blue sky.

"Goddammit John, do you smell that? Nothin' in the world like the smell of the clean fresh air."

"Yeah, it's nice. It doesn't tell me why you brought me up here." Rogers said as the wind continued to flick his stubborn strand of hair against his forehead.

"Come on over here and stand with me. Let me show you."

He did as he was told. The two together were the proverbial yin and yang. Whereas Rogers was thin and taut with deep blue sunken eyes and thin colourless lips, Simms was a giant of a man. Standing a hair over six and a half feet tall, the buttons of his shirt threatened to burst under the immense pressure of his gut. His face was chubby and despite his forty-five years, was relatively youthful, even if the crow's feet in the corners of his eyes were starting to become more prominent. He adjusted his fedora, pulling it more firmly against his head as he looked out over the lake.

"I won't lie to you John," he said with a sigh. "I wasn't going to tell you about this place. I was going to raise the money myself and take this on as a sure thing investment. Then I reminded myself that it wasn't fair, and something so certain to be a success ought to be shared with someone who can appreciate it for the opportunity it represents. You were the first name on my list."

"The fact that I'm rich enough to fund this little project had nothing to do with it I suppose?" Rogers fired back with a wry smile. He was used to situations like this. The problem with being rich was that everyone wanted to get their hands on his money. Schemes, ideas. Someone always had something to present to him.

"Come on, don't be like that. I thought we were friends?" Simms replied, not denying the accusation. "I wanted to give you the opportunity to invest. It's a completely different situation."

"You could have come to my office. Why drag me all the way out here?"

"Come on, just look at this place. You can't get the feel of it when it's just worded on paper. You have to see it. Feel it. Taste it. Experience it."

"It is beautiful up here, I'll grant you that. Makes me think twice about spoiling it by building up here."

Simms frowned and glanced at his skinny companion. "What do you mean?

"Exactly what I said. Maybe we shouldn't spoil this place."

"Don't think of it as spoiling. Try to see the vision. A year round holiday destination. People can come here to get away from the world. Imagine it. Families camping, fishing, and staying in one of our luxury cabins, all priced to be affordable to all. Like I said, it's a sure-fire winner."

"That brings me to my question."

"What question?" Bill said, his frown reappearing.

"Why so cheap? And don't give me that 'because we're friends' crap. Businessman to businessman. What's the catch?"

Simms grinned, trying to remain outwardly calm whilst his brain raced for the best way to answer. He knew getting Rogers on board was key to funding the project, and, as a result, was the most likely place it could all derail itself.

"Okay John, I'll be straight with you because I respect you as a friend and a business partner and-"

"Spit it out, Bill."

Simms took another lungful of air and watched the water, which shimmered as if filled with diamonds under the gaze of the mid-morning sun. "Alright, here it is. During our surveys, there was slight, and I do stress the word slight, risk of seismic activity in the area."

"Seismic? Are you saying you want to build in a place at risk to earthquakes?"

"No, not at all. It's not that big a risk. Just a possibility. Even so, it's not guaranteed to affect this region. The potential rewards far outweigh the risks."

"Easy for you to say when it's not your money on the line."

"John, please-"

"No, I don't think I'll be able to invest in this one. It all sounds a little bit too risky."

"As I said, the risks are minimal."

"To you maybe, but try and see it from my side. If I invest in this project now, then two or three years down the line a quake destroys the place, who do you think foots the bill? Not you, that's for sure."

"Okay, I see that. How about we renegotiate the terms of the arrangement?" Simms said, unable to quite keep the desperation out of his voice.

"I thought you said thirty percent was as high as you could go because of your 'silent' partners?"

Simms grinned, one of his big, wide friendly ones reserved exclusively for when the shit was close to hitting the fan. "Alright, say I renegotiate with them and offer you forty percent? That's a lot of long-term income."

"Sixty," Rogers said, sensing that he was now very much in the driving seat.

"I can't do sixty," Simms said, shaking his head for emphasis. "It's too high."

"Then we have nothing else to discuss. If I'm taking all the risks, I want a bigger slice of the pie." Rogers said as he started to walk away.

"What about forty-five?" Simms shouted after him.

"Sixty makes it worthwhile. Any less won't work for me."

"Come on, John, you're killing me here."

Rogers waited, watching Bill flounder by the bank of the lake.

"Alright," Simms said, knowing that any deal was better than no deal at all. "How about we go right down the middle. Fifty-fifty. Even split."

Rogers considered the proposition, deciding he could squeeze Simms for a little bit more.

"Fifty-five and we have a deal. But I'll need to get someone out to the location to independently verify this seismic activity you mentioned."

Simms chewed his lip, frowning as he shifted his weight from foot to foot. "I don't think I can go that high," he mumbled.

"Come on Bill, we both know I'm your only shot at this. Settle on giving me fifty-five, and I'll shake your hand right now."

Simms hesitated. Rogers had read him perfectly. There were no other options, and he sure as hell didn't have the cash to fund the project himself. He reminded himself that forty-five percent, although much less than he had intended on keeping, was better than nothing, which he would be looking at if Rogers walked away. With a sigh, he walked towards Rogers and thrust out a hand. "Alright, you have a deal. Damn, you're a tough negotiator. I'll get the paperwork amended at the office this afternoon."

"Not so fast," Rogers said as they shook hands. "First I want my guy out here to assess the location. I don't want to take any chances on this."

"Alright, let's get someone up here next weekend maybe. In the meantime, we can sign the paperwork."

"That won't work for me. I need to do this now. I need to fly out on business tomorrow."

"Now?" Simms repeated, checking his watch. "It's already after three. It will be dark soon. By the time we get someone up here, there won't be any time."

"I'm prepared to work late if you are. What say we get my guys out here, we verify the site, and then we can sign the agreements tomorrow morning before I leave?"

"Alright, we can do that," Simms said, hoping against hope that the people Rogers were about to call in wouldn't find anything to derail the deal. God knows he needed it to go through.

II

Simms checked his watch, grimacing at the time, which was getting close to eleven thirty. Now lit by a pale moon, the lake was no less beautiful, if a little on the cold side. They had relocated further up the valley to the proposed location of the central complex of holiday homes they planned to build. Simms's brief was simple. Do everything as cheaply as possible to maximize profits. Even though he had already agreed to give Rogers a much larger percentage of the profits than intended, he still stood to make a ton of cash just as long as Rogers signed the paperwork. Three men had arrived as per Rogers's instructions and now stood bathed in the glow of their vehicle's headlights as they probed the ground. Simms wished he knew how long such tests normally took, as he didn't know if the fact that it had already taken a long time was a good or bad thing. He walked over to the group, stopping just outside the circle of light thrown by the headlights.

"How's it going?" he asked, breath fogging in the air.

"It's looking good. We should be finished here shortly." Rogers said.

Simms nodded, immediately feeling the weight lift from his shoulders.

"There's some kind of void here." One of the surveyors said.

"Are you sure? I was assured this land was sound." Rogers replied, glancing at Simms.

"Definitely." the surveyor said, looking to Rogers for instruction.

"How deep?" Rogers asked, brow furrowed as he stared at the ground.

"Hard to say. Not without drilling into it. I can get my men up here tomorrow if you-"

The ground started to rumble, throwing up great clouds of dust and rocking the cars on their suspension.

"What the hell did you do?" Simms asked as he held onto the car for balance.

"Nothing," the surveyor shouted over the noise. "Earthquake."

Simms and Rogers retreated, scrambling for the relative safety of their vehicles. The surveyor turned to follow and then stumbled as the violent shaking continued. Simms saw it happen clearly. The ground collapsed, taking the surveyor with it. The hole started to grow bigger, dirt falling into it as it spread towards the cars. In almost perfect unison, Simms and Rogers climbed into their respective vehicles and dropped into reverse, speeding away from the ever widening hole. Rogers was terrified. Simms could only think about how he might still be able to rescue his deal. The hole widened further, throwing up great clouds of dust and sand into the air. Simms reversed his car into a gulley, slamming into a tree. He kept his foot on the accelerator, dirt was thrown up from the car as the tire continued its rotations and dug itself deeper into the soft earth. Still, the noise came the sounds of the heavens themselves opening, a thunderous roar which shook Simms and his car. He covered his head and ducked, waiting for the stomach lurching sensation of the ground falling away from under him and sending him plummeting into the darkness. He held his breath, eyes squeezed closed.

Nothing happened.

The rumble subsided and Simms exhaled, lifting his head above the level of the dashboard. His windscreen was covered with a thick film of dust, blocking his view. With a shaking hand, he activated the wipers, sweeping away the grime and revealing the outside world. Night greeted him, and for a moment, he was confused until he remembered he had reversed down the gulley, and that seeing the sky out of the window was natural under the circumstances. Still shaken, he clambered out of the car, falling to the ground on his knees and tearing his cheap suit in the process. He walked up the bank of the gully, coughing against the cloud of dust which lingered in the air. When he reached the top of the rise, he understood just how fortunate he had been. The entire flat area of land where they had moments ago been parked had disappeared, the ground collapsing into a giant void almost a hundred feet in diameter. Dust billowed out of the hole and Simms wiped a forearm against his grimy head.

"Hey Simms, you okay over there?"

Simms squinted through the dust, seeing Rogers on the opposite side of the clearing. He waved, still thinking that there might be a way to rescue the deal, even if it meant further dropping his price. "I'm fine. You?"

Rogers gave the thumbs up. "What the hell do you think caused this?" he yelled, voice echoing across the chasm.

Simms hesitated, searching for an answer that wouldn't further sour his chances of pushing the deal through and making some money. He was broken from his thought process by Rogers saying something he hadn't quite heard.

"What's what?" Simms said, straining to hear across the chasm.

"I said I can hear something moving down there. It could be Alan."

"Who?"

"Alan, my guy, the surveyor."

"Oh, right," Simms said, forgetting in the heat of the moment about how he'd been swallowed by the hole. "I don't see anything. Are you sure?"

"Not really. I can't see a damn thing down there. Do you have a flashlight?"

"I think so. Hang on."

Simms got to his feet and ducked back into the car, leaning across the seat and searching the glove box. He found the torch at the back of mountains of papers, bills and unpaid parking tickets. He hurried back to the hole, almost losing his footing on the hill.

"Alright, I got the-"

Rogers was gone. Simms scanned the perimeter of the hole, hoping he was simply out of sight. He didn't want to consider the alternative. Remembering he had the flashlight, he switched it on and scanned the opposite side of the hole, the dust dancing in the beam, which was barely strong enough to light the opposite side of the hole as is.

"John, you okay over there?" Simms shouted, his voice echoing around the hills.

He was acutely aware of the absolute silence around him. He flicked his eyes to the hole, acknowledging just how easy it would be to have slipped and fallen in. Knowing he could delay no more, he shone the beam into the hole. The torch was just as inept at dispelling the darkness as it was on the bank, making Simms half wish he had gone for the more expensive, higher quality model. He swept the beam back and forth, sure that anyone who had fallen into the chasm would surely be dead.

"John? Are you down there? Can you hear me?"

He continued to scan, then stopped and swept back. He was sure he had seen something. A shadow moving against the dark.

"John? Can you hear me?" He said, aware that his voice was barely a whisper now.

He was trying to process what he thought he'd seen. Something moving, but something big. Something impossible. He wanted to run and would have if only his car wasn't stranded. He also knew that it wouldn't take a genius to figure out his involvement, and he suspected he was already in a lot of trouble as is. At least if he tried to help, to do everything he could he might-

There.

He saw it again. A flicker of movement. Something just outside the edge of his vision. He thought he heard it this time too. A stealthy sensation of something moving.

He meant to call out again, yet the words wouldn't go past his throat. Instead, he stood there, open mouthed, pulse pounding in his temples as he scanned the black void.

He saw the flicker of mottled reddish pink just a split second before he was snatched from the edge. His torch beam danced wildly in the dusty air, before being extinguished alongside his agonized scream. For a few moments, silence followed. Then something climbed out into the night.

CHAPTER TWO

Alcatraz federal Penitentiary
   Alcatraz Island
   California

GEORGE BROWN WALKED DOWN the wide corridor, polished shoes echoing through the cavernous space. He had heard all about Alcatraz, about the kinds of people who were housed there and couldn't quite fathom why he had been dispatched to such a horrific location. Indeed, it was well known that the worst of the worst were kept here, those deemed unmanageable by other prisons and posed the greatest risk to the public. As far as he was concerned, those housed on the island could be left to rot. Although he would never say it outright, he was aggrieved at being chosen to complete this most irregular mission. More used to sitting at a desk than working out in the field, he took his handkerchief out of his pocket and dabbed his forehead, wiping away the sweat and checking that his side parted black hair was still straight and true. He arrived at the cell block gate, pausing and turning to the guard who had accompanied him.

"I can find my own way from here if you just open the door, please."

The guard, a heavy, rat-eyed man with pockmarked skin and wispy blonde hair, eyed him cautiously. "Are you sure that's a good idea, sir? It might be safer if I accompany you."

"I understand and appreciate your concern. I'll be fine."

"I understand how you might think so sir; however, this isn't just some ordinary prisoner on the other side of this gate."

"I know."

"This man is vicious. I mean, he's as bad as they come. This entire wing is reserved just for him as a precaution should he escape."

"I'm aware of Mr Rexell's history. As I'm sure you are aware sir, the warden has received our presidential order. The instructions were clear. This is a matter of the highest urgency."

"Of course, I fully understand. I was just hoping to give you a little warning, that's all."

"Duly noted officer. Now please, would you unlock the door?"

The guard stared at Brown for a moment, plainly wanting to say more but aware of the roasting the warden would give him if he did. Reluctantly, he took the keys from his belt and unlocked the gate.

"Okay sir, Rexell is on the right, the last cell down the hall. For your own safety, don't approach the bars. My name is Grant. If you have any trouble, you feel free to call out and I'll be there before you can blink."

"I understand, thank you," George said, only half hearing. His adrenaline had spiked, and he was aware of the danger that awaited him. He walked down the corridor, past the darkened rows of empty cells towards the small cone of light spilling onto the ground from the end of the hall. Shoes echoing as he walked, Brown arrived at his destination.

The cell was small, it's furnishings basic. There was a bed, a sink and a toilet. No window, just bare concrete on three sides. The tiny five by nine cell was made to look even smaller by the size of its occupant. Cody Rexell was a beast. Standing six foot five, he was a mountain of a man. He had thick black hair which touched his massive shoulders and a growth of rough stubble which was starting to grey around the chin. George stood by the cell, waiting patiently and watching as its sweaty occupant continued with his workout routine, performing press ups with piston accuracy. He showed no sign of tiring as he continued, nose to the ground, and full extension of his sweat-slicked muscled arms. George was aware he had been seen. It was impossible not to be, his shoes almost directly in Rexell's eye line, yet the giant went on. Up, down. Up, down. Up down.

George counted a further thirty repetitions before Rexell stopped and hopped to his feet. He glared at George, breathing heavily from his efforts, blue eyes harsh and uninviting, white scar cutting through his eyebrow standing out clearly as he turned away from his visitor and wiped an arm against his forehead. He walked to the sink and turned it on, cupping his hands and filling them with water which he slurped down. George stood in the corridor and shuffled his feet, unsure quite how to proceed now that he was standing in front of one of the country's most dangerous men.

"Who are you?" Rexell asked, his voice deep and filled with the same menace as his eyes as he sat on the edge of his bunk, sweat dripping onto the floor.

"Good day to you, Mr Rexell, my name is George Brown. I work for the United States government."

"Whatever you're here to accuse me of, I probably did it."

"I'm not here to accuse you of anything, sir. I was sent to ask for your help."

Rexell looked at George from where he was perched on the bed, elbows on knees, head hanging low. "Are you serious?"

"Very. I'm here by order of the President himself."

"Really? And what would Dwight want with a vagrant like me?"

"President Eisenhower needs you to use your, uh, specific skill set to help with a problem we recently encountered in Montana."

"Not interested."

"I haven't explained the situation yet, Mr Rexell."

"I'll save you the trouble. I don't want to know. You say you know all about me and why I'm here. If that's true, then you know there's no chance of me ever seeing the outside of this hell hole again."

"I'm aware of your reasons for being here, Mr Rexell. Assault. Fraud. Murder. Frankly, you were lucky to avoid the chair."

"My lawyer is good. What can I say? Even so, this place ain't no picnic. But you're right. I did all those things, and now I'm paying for it."

"You don't seem too concerned about your predicament," Brown said, surprised at how articulate Rexell was.

"I'm six years into a forty stretch. What else do you expect me to say?"

Brown stepped closer to the cell, almost putting his face between the bars. "What if I could guarantee your freedom?"

Rexell took his eyes off the floor and set them on Brown. "I'd say you were talking shit."

"Hear me out. If you agree to help with this situation, I can secure you a presidential release from custody for the duration of the mission, followed by a transfer out of Alcatraz to a more comfortable prison. Even you have to admit Mr Rexell that it will make the rest of those forty years a lot easier to handle."

Rexell stood, extending to his full height, causing Brown to step back away from the bars. He held out his arm, which was covered with tattoos. "You see that tat there?"

Brown looked where Rexell was pointing. It was of a woman, a busty pinup sitting provocatively on the underside of his forearm. Beneath it, inked in an ugly shaky font, perhaps by Rexell himself, were three letters.

B.M.F

"Do you know what that means, Mr. Government man?"

Brown shook his head. "No, I'm afraid I don't."

"That stands for bad motherfucker, which is exactly what I am. If you came here trying to tempt me with a life away from Alcatraz, then you're wasting your time. I can handle it here. I've been in some of the worst hellholes in the world. Places that would make you shit your pants and run screaming back to your nice cosy office job. Believe me, after some of the things I've seen, this place is easy."

"You haven't heard me out."

"I don't need to." Rexell fired back, sitting back on his bunk, which creaked in protest. "If Dwight needs my help, whatever it might be for, then he can get his presidential ass down here and ask me in person."

"I'm afraid that's quite impossible, Mr Rexell. President Eisenhower is a very busy man."

"Then you and me have nothin else to talk about."

"I'm sure when you understand the gravity of the situation-"

He moved fast, much quicker than Brown could ever have anticipated. Before he could step away from the bars, Rexell was on him. He pulled Brown's left arm into the cell, bending it back against the steel to the point where it could easily be broken. At the same time, he reached through with his right arm and grabbed Brown on the back of the neck, pulling his face to the cell, smashing his nose and face against the bars. Brown grunted and snorted as blood from his broken nose began to stain his suit.

"Now you listen to me and you listen well," Rexell growled, their foreheads almost touching on opposite sides of the steel. "I don't like repeating myself, so I'm going to say this once and once only. I'm an impatient man. I don't like authority; I also don't like people trying to tell me what to do. If Dwight is too busy to come and ask me himself to do whatever it is he wants me to do, then I don't see that as valuable enough to waste my time on. Now you run along back to Washington and tell him that. I'll be here waiting for him if he changes his mind."

Brown squirmed against the bars, eyes wide with fear. Rexell grinned.

"Don't worry. I ain't gonna hurt you. I'm just proving a point that's all. I could break you right now. Snap your arm. Break your neck. It would be easy. I won't do that because I know why you're here. You were sent to me because I'm the only one like me in the world. I do the shit that other people can't get done. But if you want me to help you, if our President wants my help, then he's gonna have to come here and ask me in person. I want to smell the fear on him like I can smell it on you, understood?"

"Yesh, yesh I undhershthandh," Brown said, his face still mashed against the bars.

Rexell released him, smiling as Brown lurched back, putting his hands to his bloody face.

"Good," Rexell said, sitting back on the edge of his bunk, completely calm. "Now you go back and tell him what I said."

Brown didn't argue. He hurried down the corridor, blood streaming from his face as Rexell's laughter echoed behind him.

II

Twenty-six hours later, Rexell was still sitting in the hole, Alcatraz's pet name for solitary confinement. The tiny cell was pitch dark and offered barely enough room to move. Warden James hadn't taken the news of Rexell's treatment of Brown well and had immediately had him sent to solitary to think about the situation he had put the prison in. Although to most, spending so much time in a cold, lightless tiny space would be as hellish as it was intended to be. Rexell, however, actually liked it. The dark was, at least, a change of scenery from his cell, and it helped him to think and stay focused. He was a semi-regular visitor, and no matter how long his stay he always came out refreshed and happy, much to the anger and frustration of the warden. As he lay in the dark, he heard the door scrape open, letting golden artificial light claw its way into his world. He squinted at the doorframe, waiting for his eyes to adjust.

He blinked once.

Twice.

Yet he still couldn't quite believe what he was seeing. Standing there surrounded by light and flanked by his security team, stood President Dwight Eisenhower.

"Come with me, Mr Rexell," The President said. "You and I need to talk."

III

Twenty minutes later, Cody Rexell sat in the warden's office, looking across the table at the most powerful man in America. Warden James fidgeted by the door, keeping an equally watchful eye on the president's staff. His discomfort pleased Rexell immensely.

"So, you're telling me you discovered some kind of monster, and you want me to kill it?"

"That's correct." The President replied, keeping eye contact with Rexell.

"Why me?"

"Excuse me?"

"I said, why me? Surely, you have the best of everything. Weapons. Resources. Soldiers. You control the entire damn country."

"Watch your mouth, boy." One of the security team snapped.

The president held up a hand. "It's alright; Mr Rexell poses a valid question. Why you indeed."

The President leafed through the overstuffed folder on the desk. Rexell craned his neck to watch, handcuffs clinking behind his back. "Your file makes interesting reading."

"Thanks."

"Extortion, assault, kidnapping. Robbery. Vandalism. Drunk driving. Public lewdness."

"You're making me blush, Mr President."

"It also says here you are highly skilled. An expert in martial arts, warfare. It also says you were involved in suspected arms dealing and have a vast knowledge of weaponry, both legal and otherwise. Is this true?"

"That depends. Will it add to my sentence?"

"What you say here, Mr Rexell remains off the record."

"Then maybe it is. Let's just say I know how to handle myself."

"It also says here that you served in the army before things went sour. What happened there?"

Rexell shrugged. "I didn't like it. I don't work well with authority, just ask the warden here." He tipped Warden James a wink as he said it, receiving a glare which would sour milk in response.

President Eisenhower closed the file, resting his manicured hands on the table top. "I'm going to level with you. This creature which was uncovered by the earthquake is unlike anything we have ever seen before. Fortunately, it has remained territorial to the area where it was uncovered, but people will eventually start to ask questions. We need someone with your, uh, unique skills to deal with this problem. This is a hell of a chance for you to redeem yourself Mr Rexell. A hell of a chance to start sleeping well at night again and with a clear conscience."

"Well, Mr President here's the problem. Maybe I don't want redemption. Maybe I sleep fine as is. And maybe, just maybe, moving from one shithole prison to another isn't incentive enough for me to consider your proposal."

"You don't say no to me. I'm the goddamn president." Eisenhower said, glaring across the table

"Not of me. It's all well and good you coming here now when you need something. We both know you'd have left me here to rot until the end of time if this thing hadn't crawled out of the ground."

"So you're saying you won't help us? Won't help your country?"

"I didn't say that. This is just about negotiating. It's a fringe benefits kind of situation. If I'm going to do this, and that's a big if, it's gonna take a hell of a lot more than a prison transfer to do it."

"I'm not in the business of negotiating, Mr Rexell."

"And I'm not in the business of working for free."

"I don't see how you have any bargaining power here. Frankly, I'm shocked that you seem so lax about this situation. This is a potential threat to the safety of our country. God knows what will happen when this thing decides to go further than this hole in the ground and encounters people, towns, and cities. It would be a bloodbath."

"Why don't you just send a team down there and kill this thing? I'm struggling to understand the confusion."

The president shifted in his seat, hesitating before turning to one of his men stationed by the door. "Send George in with the file."

The hulking guard did as he was asked. Rexell watched as his visitor from the previous day – now sporting two fabulously painful looking black eyes and a bandage on his nose walked into the office, giving Rexell a wide berth. He handed the president another folder, this one with the words TOP SECRET: EYES ONLY stamped on it in red.

Rexell craned his neck to try and see as the president opened the file. Eisenhower saw him and motioned to one of the two men standing behind Cody's chair.

"Take those cuffs off him."

"Sir, I don't think that's a good idea," George said, glaring at Cody who met his gaze with a dead man's stare designed to intimidate.

"I didn't ask your opinion, George, I gave an order. Un-cuff him."

The men beside Rexell's chair complied, removing the handcuffs. Rexell rubbed his wrists and tipped a wink at George, who looked like he would rather be anywhere else in the world. The president tossed the secret file across the desk.

"Go ahead and take a look. Maybe it might sway you."

Rexell leafed through the file, storing information, looking for anything he might use as the president talked him through it.

"Immediately following the disturbance in Montana, local police attended the scene after a helicopter reported vehicles by the hole. The two officers who went to investigate were taken by this thing. We believe the occupants of the two vehicles suffered the same fate.

"Taken?" Rexell said, looking up from the file.

"We don't believe this thing is killing people yet, but using them."

"For what?"

"Frankly, we don't know. We know they're alive as we can still hear them down there. We assume that it's one of two scenarios. Either this thing is storing those it takes as a food source for later, which means it will venture out into the world when those supplies run out."

"What's the second scenario?"

"That this creature is using these people to house its young. At best guess, this creature is some kind of worm. Some species gestate their eggs in live hosts. This could become an epidemic."

"I still don't understand why you want me to do this. What's the angle here?"

Eisenhower looked around the room at the half dozen security guards. "Everybody out."

"Sir-"

"Not now George. That's a direct order. Out. Everyone."

They filed out of the room, leaving the president and Rexell alone.

The President waited until the door was closed. "Alright, here's the deal. We tried to stop this thing. We threw everything we could at it. It has some kind of armour plating running across the top of its body. Our bullets don't affect it, grenades and explosives ineffective. Now I know you have contacts out in the world, people who can acquire you weapons which might be effective against this thing that for various political and moral reasons we can't get ourselves."

"I don't know what you're talking about," Rexell said, locking eyes with the president. "Even if I did, I couldn't make contact with those people from in here."

"Let's cut out the bullshit. Even though it couldn't be proven at trial, we know you have contacts in the weapons industry. The Mexicans speak highly of you, they talk like you're some kind of god to them. A legend. We also know you have access to Russian technology too. Experimental weaponry, advanced warfare tools which might give us a chance against this thing. Now I'm putting all my cards on the table here in the interests of protecting this country. Let it be made clear that I didn't want to come to you with this. You're volatile and unpredictable. Dangerous. A potential headache."

"This isn't the best way to talk me into bed with you, Mr President."

"Let me finish. You're also known to be uncompromising. Fearless. Willing to do things that an ordinary man wouldn't. You also have the contacts that we don't. You fit in with the others like you. The scum of the earth. The seedy, vile, disgusting people who can maybe give you what you need to make this situation go away. The truth is, when researched who would be best suited to do this one of a kind mission, yours was the only name that came up."

"I'm glad you're aware of my work. I'm also glad that you know how good I am. Because of that, the cost of my services has just gone up."

"Cost? You want money?"

Rexell laughed. "Believe me, I have money. None that your government would ever find or be able to trace to me, but more than enough."

"You might think so, Mr Rexell. But we could give you a real payday. Enough to set you up for life, enough so that when you eventually secured your release from prison, you wouldn't need to live a life of crime. You could integrate back into society."

"I don't think you quite understand Mr President. How much money were you talking about as my retainer for this mission of yours?"

"One hundred thousand dollars. Tax-free. Yours in full on completion of the mission, if you survive."

"Five million."

"Excuse me?" The president said, "That's ridiculous. We could never afford it."

"No, that's not what I want. It's how much I have out there, scattered around in places you will never find it. Keep your hundred grand. I don't need it."

Eisenhower shuffled in his seat and cleared his throat. "So what do you want?"

"Well, Mr President," Rexell said, leaning back and putting his feet up on the table. "My needs are quite simple. As I said, I don't need money. What I want is out of here. Out of this stinking prison."

"As we said, you would be transferred to a medium security facility. Given many privileges to make the remainder of your sentence much more comfortable. I understand you still have a significant term to serve."

"No. I'm not interested in a transfer."

"Then what the hell do you want?"

"I want my freedom. I want a full pardon for any crimes proved or assumed. I also want immunity from future arrest."

"Impossible. I can't authorize that." Eisenhower said, staring wide-eyed across the table.

"That's up to you. If you're right about this worm looking to spread its species, then you might want to consider what's most important to you. Upsetting your people or letting this worm eat everyone alive. It makes no difference to me either way."

"You don't seem to understand. If that happens, you'll be at risk too. This could change the way our species lives."

"Unless this thing can swim, I think I'll be fine right here in Alcatraz."

"Mr Rexell, please be reasonable. You can't expect me to give you immunity. You're a danger to the public. It would be morally wrong."

"I understand that. You have to ask yourself now, Mr President, which of us causes the bigger threat to your country. Is it me, or this creature?"

The President sighed and rubbed his temples. "Let's say I could make this happen. What else would you need?"

"Nothing apart from full authority to do whatever I need to do. I don't want police interfering with my work. Remember, you're hiring me because I work in a unique way. It might not be what you and your people are expecting. I don't want every officer between here and Montana harassing me at every turn."

"I can't just release you into the world and trust your word. I need some kind of assurance that you're doing the job. I'll need to have a chaperone go with you. We'll also need to put a tracker of some kind on you so we know where you are at all times."

"You can do that?"

"We have the technology, yes."

"I can live with that. I'll also need a blind eye to be turned for the length of the mission."

"I don't think I understand."

Rexell smiled and took his feet off the desk. "As you said yourself, I know some pretty bad people who don't need the attention of the government. They trust me because I'm one of them. What I don't need is for them to start being arrested after I visit them. They need to be left alone no matter what your chaperone sees or hears."

"Okay Mr Rexell, it's obvious you're interested in this. And you're plainly the right man for the job. Although I might be able to accommodate some of your requests, I'm afraid there's no way I can pardon you. I just can't do it. You must understand my position here."

"Then we have no deal."

"Let me finish. The governor tells me you're here awaiting execution."

"Not exactly. There's another trial trying to pin a murder on me, which, for the record, I didn't do. If they convict me of it, then yeah, chances are I'll get the chair."

"Then how about this. You complete the mission, using all of our vast resources in whatever way you see fit. In return, you will be moved to a medium-security prison where you will live in relative luxury. After say, five or six years, we will quietly release you with a new identity. No death penalty. No new trial. All of that will go away."

"What if I don't want a new identity?"

"Listen, son," The president said, slamming his fist on the desk. "You need to start thinking smart. It says here you're an intelligent guy, so I'll say this once. You can either do this and show a bit of goodwill towards your country and go on to live the rest of your life in relative freedom, or you can fry in that chair and leave this world behind, and, believe me, you will fry, sooner rather than later. I'll make sure of that. To me, it seems like a very simple decision."

Rexell grinned. "Death doesn't scare me. And I don't get intimidated. You'll have to try harder than that."

"Well, what do you want dammit?"

"I already told you. I'll kill this creature for you. In return, I walk away a free man with my record wiped clean. No new identity. No medium security prison. With all due respect, Mr President, you need me more than I need you, which makes this particular agreement non-negotiable. Now are we going to sit here and bicker about it, or are you going to let me go out there and do what I do better than anyone else in the world?"

Eisenhower was furious. He sat for a moment, drumming his fingers on the table top. "Alright, you win. If you complete this mission, and by that I mean kill this creature, I'll set you free. You have my word."

"Then, Mr President, you have yourself a deal. When do I start?"

"Right away. We need this contained before the public finds out about it. We have a chopper ready to fly you out of here to a facility where your tracker will be fitted."

"I don't want anything too heavy. I need to be able to move around."

"It's a small device. It will be stitched in under the skin of your forearm. You won't even know it's there."

Rexell grinned. "You never had any doubt I'd accept, did you?"

The president shook his head. "Not once. Your belongings are already packed and waiting for you on board. We leave in ten minutes."

"Where are we going?"

"I want you to see what you're up against."

"A personal tour by the president? Not bad at all."

"Sadly not. I have to get back to D.C. I'll be monitoring the situation from there. My chief of staff, Pertwee, will take you to the site and assist you in whatever way you need after you have visited the location. He will also be your chaperone for the duration of the operation and be reporting directly to me. After you have seen what you are up against, the next move is up to you."

"Alright," Rexell said, standing. "Then let's get moving."

"One more thing, Mr Rexell. I need to make it clear to you that this mission is one in which we can't offer you military support. It's important we remain as covert as possible. Also, once the flyby is over and you have given the first instruction, you are completely on your own."

"What you're saying is, I'm expendable?"

The president looked Rexell in the eye. "Yes, that's what I'm saying. I'm also telling you that this is all in. If you kill this thing, then you will go free. However, if you fail and this thing isn't destroyed, if you try to run or escape without doing as you have agreed, you'll be back here before your bed can get cold. Understood?"

Rexell nodded. "Crystal clear Mr President. Crystal clear."

"Good. Now get the hell out of here."

CHAPTER THREE

THE BLACK HELICOPTER CUT through the crisp morning air, the greens and browns of Montana flashing beneath them. Finally out of his prison-issue clothes and dressed in jeans, a black t-shirt and roughed up leather jacket, Rexell looked at the cavernous opening below.

"That's its lair," Pertwee said, his voice crackling over the headphones.

Rexell stared at it, surprised at just how big it was. He could see a network of tunnels snaking through the rock, but no sign of the creature itself.

"Where is it?"

"It seems to be nocturnal for the most part. Light sensitive." the chubby official said, shifting in his seat, blue eyes looking past Rexell rather than at him.

Rexell nodded and turned back to the window. "Why is the perimeter so far back?"

"The creature senses vibrations. If we get within a hundred feet or so of the hole, it senses our movements and attacks."

"Great."

"You didn't think this would be easy did you?" Pertwee said.

Rexell didn't answer the question. Instead, he responded with one of his own. "Why not drop some explosives down there? Surely that would be enough to get the job done."

"The hole there is just its entry and exit point. Those tunnels could go for miles underground, so this creature could be anywhere. Besides, this area is highly seismic. We don't want to do anything to trigger another quake, so explosives are off the table."

"That was never mentioned."

"You think if this was as easy as dropping a bomb down there we would have needed you?"

Rexell grunted and stared into the black abyss. "Alright, I've seen enough. I need to get down on the ground."

"What's your plan?" Pertwee asked.

"Nothing yet. I need to go to Texas and see a friend of mine."

"Texas? I don't think so. You were tasked with destroying this creature, not travelling halfway across the country so you can buddy up with a pal of yours."

Rexell turned in his seat, staring at Pertwee. "We do this my way. That was the deal."

"My job is to keep you focused. This isn't a holiday."

"We go to Texas."

"No, we don't."

"I'm not asking."

"I'm in charge here."

"Look pal, unless you expect me to jump in there and drag this thing out with my bare hands, you better listen to what I have to say. I was told we do this my way or not at all. Now I get that you don't like me. Frankly, I don't give a shit. You either do as I tell you, or you can take me back to The Rock right now."

Pertwee squirmed in his seat, upper lip twitching as he stared first at, and then past Rexell at the pastel blue sky outside.

"Fine. Texas it is. For the record, since we're being honest, let me tell you how things are from my point of view. I don't like you. I also think it's a mistake to be bringing you out here. You're a bad penny, and I don't think you're looking out for anyone but yourself. Having said that, the president has decided he wants you to do this, and so I have to go along with it. Just know that I'm watching your every move, and the first whiff of something I don't like, you'll be back to that cell of yours quicker than a hiccup. Understood?"

Rexell stared at Pertwee for a few seconds, then grinned. "That's the first thing you've said so far that hasn't sounded like Americana bullshit. How does it feel to be honest for a change?"

"It's not hard when it concerns scum like you."

"You call me scum. Others might call me a war hero. Either way, I don't care. Believe it or not, I'm a man of my word Pertwee. You do as I tell you to do and keep quiet the rest of the time, then the two of us will get on just fine. If you don't, then I won't be responsible for what happens to you. Do you understand that?"

"I guess so."

"Good. Then do me a favour. Tell the pilot to get us on the ground and let's get our asses to Texas."

CHAPTER FOUR

San Antonio,
    Texas

THE DINER WAS ALIVE with chatter, the counter and red
leather-backed booths almost filled to capacity. Waitresses
flitted between tables, taking orders, serving drinks ranging
from beer to hot coffee to the backdrop of rockabilly music
pumping from the jukebox in the corner.

"This is a waste of time. What the hell are we doing here?"
Pertwee asked, glaring at Rexell across the table as he cut into
the giant steak on his plate.

"I'm hungry."

"We don't have time for this. We can't afford to wait any
longer."

Rexell set his knife and fork down and sipped his beer.
"Relax. It's all in control."

"From where I'm sitting, nothing is in control. Why the
hell have you dragged us all the way out here?"

"I like this place. I used to eat here all the time."

Pertwee leaned close, the ugly vein in his temple pulsing.
"Look," he whispered. "You need to get with the program here.
You know how important this mission is. Time is critical. This
isn't some kind of damn holiday from prison."

"Relax," Rexell replied, barely paying any attention as he
looked past Pertwee to the waitress a few booths away. The four
men there – all clad in matching black jackets and greasy, jet

black haircuts were teasing her as she tried to take their order, grabbing at her legs and making her life hard.

"Hey, are you even listening to me?" Pertwee grunted.

Rexell didn't answer. He slowly sipped his beer, watching the greasers giving the waitress a hard time. He could see why she was getting the attention. She was tall and slim, with red hair and sharp green eyes. Although she was taking their teasing well, the frustration was obviously growing.

"Wait here a second," Rexell said, taking another sip of his beer then sliding out of the booth.

"Where the hell do you think you're going?"

Rexell didn't answer. He walked towards the waitress. "Why don't you leave her alone?"

The four greasers stared at Rexell, arrogant grins frozen in place.

"Who the hell are you?" One of them said, looking Rexell up and down.

"It doesn't matter. I'm telling you to leave the lady alone."

"You're telling us what?" The greasers were staring at him like a pack of wild dogs.

Rexell stood limp, arms at his sides, aware that all chatter in the diner had ceased. "Look, this doesn't have to get ugly. Just do as I say."

"Can you believe this guy?" One of them said, clearly enjoying the attention. "My buddies and me were just talking to the waitress here. What does it have to do with you?"

"Maybe you and your buddies ought to finish up and leave. You're disturbing my meal."

The ringleader flicked an alligator smile, showing perfect white teeth as his buddies cheered him on. "I don't know how well you count, pal, but we outnumber you four to one. Maybe you should go back to your table before you get yourself hurt."

As he said it, he set a switchblade on the table, tapping it with a pale, bony index finger.

"Kid, you don't wanna go down this road," Rexell said, staring him dead in the eye.

"I ain't no kid. If you want trouble, we'll be happy to help you find it."

Rexell weighed them up. They were in their late teens, maybe early twenties. Their matching jacket and haircuts only went so far into building their tough guy personas. On closer inspection, their eyes were frightened behind the macho expressions, and Rexell was sure an example, although potentially painful, might be in order to calm the situation before they started waving their knives around and did something stupid.

"This is your last chance," He said, making a mental note of his surroundings, playing out everything he was about to do in his mind. There was absolute silence from the patrons in the diner, and only the jukebox continued to blast out Frankie Avalon's hit song Venus.

"Stick him, Charlie," one of the ringleader's friends said without conviction.

"Yeah, Charlie," Rexell echoed. "Stick me. See what happens." Rexell leaned on the table, inching closer to Charlie, making sure to position his hands in such a way so that he would be in easy reach of one of the knives on the table with his left hand and the kid closest to Charlie with his right. Rexell gave Charlie the thousand yard stare, hoping it would be enough to make them back off. As much as he could finish them with ease, he didn't particularly feel like breaking bones so early in the day, especially on such a nice morning.

"How about it, Charlie? I haven't got all day. Make your move and let's do this." Rexell said.

Charlie squirmed, his Adam's apple dancing in his throat. Rexell could read him perfectly. He was scared, and it was clear that he didn't want to react, but at the same time, his friends were there and sometimes, in Rexell's experience, that made people do stupid things.

"Hey man, let's just get out of here." One of his friends whispered. Both Rexell and Charlie ignored him. It was as if nothing existed but the two of them.

Charlie blinked, and in that one instant, Rexell knew he had won.

"Yeah, screw this place," Charlie said, sliding out of the booth, swiftly followed by his friends. They walked to the door, full of swagger and bravado, desperately trying to save face. "I don't wanna eat in a hole like this anyway," Charlie said as he pushed through the door. Rexell watched as they fired up their motorcycles and left the parking lot in a cloud of screeching tires and smoke. With them, they took the tension, and chatter returned to the diner. Rexell returned to his seat, ignoring the cautious gaze of the staff and customers as he sat opposite Pertwee.

"What the hell was all that about?" Pertwee whispered. "We're supposed to be keeping a low profile here."

"They walked out of here didn't they?"

"Yes but-"

"I consider that keeping a low profile compared to how ugly it would have got if they had made a move."

Before Pertwee could formulate a reply, the redheaded waitress who had been the subject of the harassment came over to the table. She looked even better up close, and Rexell couldn't help but notice just how brilliant her eyes were.

"Thanks for that," she said, setting another beer on the table.

"Uh, ma'am, we didn't order more drinks," Pertwee said.

"On the house, for your friend here for helping me out." She smiled at Rexell, a gesture he was more than happy to return.

"Thanks, I appreciate it..." he made a show of leaning forward to look at her name badge even though he had already seen it when he first went to assist her. "Marion."

"No problem, you really helped me out. Those guys are in here all the time, pawing at me. I hate it."

"I don't think they'll come back again, not for a while at least."

"Still, I really do appreciate it."

"Don't worry about it, thanks for the beer," Rexell said, flashing her a smile.

She hovered by the table, shifting her weight from foot to foot. "So...I haven't seen you around before. You new in town?" She asked.

"You could say that. I'm here on business."

"What kind of business?"

"Well, there's this big ass monster I'm supposed to hunt down and kill-"

"Okay, okay," Pertwee cut in, faking a laugh as he stared at Rexell. "He's joking of course. We're just passing through. We're property developers."

Marion frowned, looking from Pertwee in his pristine suit to Rexell in his boots, jeans, dirty t-shirt and leather jacket.

"You don't look like a property developer," She said, focusing her attention on Rexell.

"I'm not," Rexell said back with a smile, enjoying watching Pertwee squirm. "Neither is he."

"Look, we should be going," Pertwee said, starting to get up.

"I'm still finishing my steak," Rexell said, making no effort to move. "And I'm talking to Marion here."

"We have to go," Pertwee said through gritted teeth.

"Sit down."

Pertwee hesitated, then did as he was told, face screwed up as if he were chewing a wasp.

"Sorry about that," Rexell said to Marion, back in full charm mode. "I don't think I introduced myself. I'm Cody." He held out a hand. She shook it, her skin soft against his rough palm.

"Nice to meet you," she said, lowering her eyes to the table for a second, then turning them back on him.

"Like my friend said, we have to go right now, but, I could maybe take you out for a drink sometime?"

"Yeah, I'd like that."

"Alright, then I guess I'll see you again soon." He slid out of the booth, keeping his eyes on her as he drained his beer.

"When?" She asked.

"Soon," Rexell said, winking at her as he walked towards the door, conscious of the stares of the other diners as he made his leave.

"Can we get on with why we are here now?" Pertwee said as he followed, walking briskly to keep up.

"Soon. First I have one more stop to make."

CHAPTER FIVE

DUSK FINALLY BROUGHT SOME relief from the scorching heat of the day. Some five miles outside of San Antonio, the blue government car came to a halt, dust puffing up around its tires. Rexell got out, followed by Pertwee. The car ticked as it cooled, the only other sound that of Rexell's boots as he walked into the desert.

"Hey, where the hell do you think you're going?" Pertwee said, jogging to catch up.

He glanced at their surroundings, which comprised of sand as far as the eye could see, broken up by the occasional sprig of green which tried to defy the odds by existing in such a hostile environment. Rexell came to a halt, planting his fists on his hips and staring out into the wilderness.

"Don't even think about running," Pertwee said.

Rexel held up his bandaged forearm. "Even if I wanted to I couldn't. You have your little tracker in me, remember?"

"Well if it's not to run, then who come out here."

"I told you. I needed to make one more stop."

"There's nobody here," Pertwee hissed. "You better not be wasting our time."

Rexell put an index finger in each corner of his mouth and whistled, the sound rolling into the vast desert. "Calm down Pertwee. I know what I'm doing."

"This is a joke. We don't have time for this." Pertwee hissed.

"Shut up and hold your water," Rexell grunted.

A small plume of dust rolled from the horizon, angling towards where the two of them stood.

"What the hell is that?" Pertwee asked.

"Just wait."

They watched as the plume came closer. Pertwee saw what it was, and started to back off towards the car.

"Don't move," Rexell said, not taking his eyes off the approaching cloud.

The Alsatian was huge, muscles bunched as it sprinted towards them. Its eyes glared with venomous intent, and its teeth were slick with saliva.

Pertwee looked from the approaching dog to Rexell, trying to read him and finding that his profile betrayed little.

"Get ready," Rexell whispered, setting his feet in the dirt. "This could get ugly."

Pertwee stepped back as the dog leapt at them, drool flicking from its jaws. It landed on Rexell, knocking him to the ground, snarling and snapping at his face as the two rolled in the dirt.

"Jesus!" Pertwee screamed, unsure what to do. It was then he realised that the dog wasn't biting Rexell, but licking him. Pertwee looked on as Rexell cooed and scratched the dog behind the ears, letting it lick and slobber all over his face. Eventually, he stood, the dog sitting in front of him, panting and watching its master.

"This is Magnum," Rexell said as he wiped the drool from his face.

"I thought it was going to attack you," Pertwee muttered, adjusting his tie.

"Not a chance. Magnum has saved my life more times than I can remember."

Pertwee looked at the dog. Its fur was pocked with scars and old wounds long healed.

"Hey boy," Pertwee said, reaching out to stroke Magnum's head.

The dog snarled and snapped, barking at Pertwee and showing its teeth.

"That's a good way to lose a finger or two," Rexell said, watching as the dog inched towards Pertwee, who in turn stepped back, his legs banging into the car.

"Call it off," He whispered, too afraid to take his eyes off the animal. "Damn it Rexell, call it off."

Rexell waited just a few seconds longer, then broke into a grin. "Leave it Magnum."

The dog obeyed; returning to its position in front of its master, tail swishing, tongue lolling as it waited to be told what to do.

"That thing isn't safe," Pertwee grunted, wiping sweat from his forehead. "And it's too damn hot out here. What are we supposed to be waiting for?"

"We need supplies. Weapons to take down this worm of yours."

"So what now, is the damn dog going to provide them for you?"

"Actually, he is," Rexell said, scratching the animal behind the ear. "Magnum, go find Spike."

The dog barked once and trotted towards the edge of the road.

"You wait here with the car. I'll be back by dawn." Rexell started to walk towards the desert, the dog bounding in front of him as Pertwee followed.

"You don't expect me to just let you walk away from here do you?"

Rexell stopped and turned to face Pertwee. "I told you. I'll be back by dawn."

"Not a chance. What, I'm supposed to just let you go and then never see you again? You think I was born yesterday?"

"I don't know what you want me to say. I can't take you with me. I'm wearing the damn tracker, it's not like I can go anywhere."

"Why not, why can't I come along?"

"My friend is a very untrusting man. He doesn't take kindly to strangers, let alone government officials. Now if you want me to kill this beast of yours, you need to let me go and see him alone."

"I'm sorry, I can't do that," Pertwee said, grabbing Rexell by the arm. Magnum growled low in his throat, ears back against his head as he inched towards Pertwee.

"You might want to let go of me. Magnum gets a little overprotective."

"Look, you have to understand, you're putting me in an impossible situation here. I have orders from the President for God's sake."

Magnum continued to growl and drool in the sand, back legs tense and ready to pounce on Pertwee. The two men locked eyes, and Rexell broke into a grin.

"Alright, then we do it your way."

"Good. Do you want to call your damn dog off now?" Pertwee said, a light sweat on his brow. Rexell turned to the dog and flicked his head. The dog stopped growling and padded away from the two men, keeping a watchful eye on

Pertwee as it circled at the edge of the road. The government official released his grip on Rexell and stood straight, loosening his tie.

"Alright, you come with me. You keep your mouth shut and let me do the talking. And for your own sake, I wouldn't mention that you are with the government, although..."

Rexell took a step back and looked Pertwee up and down. "Yeah, you look the part. You have government stooge written all over you. Lose the tie and the jacket. It's hot out here anyway, you'll thank me for it."

"I have air conditioning in the car," Pertwee said, unwilling to acknowledge that Rexell was right.

"We're not going in the car. We're going on foot."

"Out there? Are you crazy?" Pertwee said, staring into the desolate desert. "We have no water. There's nothing out there."

Rexell grinned. "You know, it's because of stupid people like you that people like me can keep our shit hidden and away from prying eyes."

"What do you mean by that?"

"Stupid people, Pertwee. I mean stupid people. Just because you can't see it, doesn't mean there's nothing out there."

"This is a bad idea," Pertwee grumbled.

Rexell shrugged. Despite the heat, he looked completely unaffected. He stared at Pertwee, eyes cold and indifferent. "It's up to you. By all means, stay here with the car. I'm going to find my friend."

Rexell turned to Magnum, who was standing patiently by the side of the road. "Go find Spike."

The dog reacted immediately, bounding off into the desert. Rexell followed, side stepping down the embankment from the road and setting out on foot after the dog, which stopped every twenty feet or so to wait for its master before running further ahead. Pertwee stood on the sun-baked asphalt, looking up and down the deserted stretch of highway. The blazing sun glittered off the chrome bodywork of his car, hurting his eyes. He looked at Rexell, who was disappearing into the distance.

"Goddamn it," he grunted, then took off his tie and jacket, tossed them into the car and followed Rexell and Magnum into the desert.

II

They walked for what felt like an eternity. Pertwee was already drenched in sweat, his shirt sticking to his back and reminding him that he had spent too long sitting on his ass and working in an office than actually being out in the field. Rexell seemed unaffected. He followed Magnum, who seemed to be wandering aimlessly into the endless stretch of sand. Pertwee looked over his shoulder, distressed to see that the road and his car was no longer visible apart from the occasional shimmer of light as the sun flashed across the bodywork.

"How much longer," Pertwee grunted, his throat already as dry as the sand at his feet.

"Not sure. Until Magnum lets us know we're where we need to be."

"You put a lot of trust in that animal."

"I trust it more than any human I know."

"Look pal, maybe you put your faith in some dumb animal, I don't. The damn thing doesn't have a clue where it's going. It's as lost as we are."

Rexell wasn't paying attention. He was watching Magnum. The dog had come to a stop at the edge of a ridge, limbs tense, tail stiff between its legs.

"Wait here," Rexell said, crouching and inching forward. For once, Pertwee did as he was told, hanging back as Rexell moved beside Magnum.

The desert floor dropped away into a natural bowl of sorts, surrounded on three sides by craggy rock outcrops. The dirty motorhome was parked against the rear of the bowl in the shade of one of the rock outcrops. A red truck was parked beside it.

The motorhome and truck belonged to Spike, Rexell knew that for a fact. What he didn't understand was why Magnum was so spooked.

"What is it, boy?" Rexell whispered as he crouched beside the dog. "Where's Spike?"

The dog growled low in its throat, then whined and snorted, before lowering itself to the ground. Rexell watched and waited, trusting the animal's instincts. He didn't have to wait for long. The sound came to him first, rolling through the hot desert air to where they waited.

Engines. Three at least. He hunkered down, making sure he was out of sight. He saw the plume of dust first, a great rooster tail curling into the pale blue sky. The truck came first, bounding over the uneven terrain towards the motorhome. The three motorcycles trailed behind, and even from a distance, Rexell recognised the riders.

"What's happening?" Pertwee said as he crawled on his belly beside Rexell, making sure to keep his distance from Magnum.

"Recognize our friends?" Rexell said, watching as the truck and three bikes came to a stop outside the motorhome.

"Those kids from the diner," Pertwee said.

"Yeah. I'm not sure who that is with them, though."

Unlike the bikers, the driver of the truck was older, and even from a distance, Rexell could see just how big he was. He spilled out of the truck, a mountain of flesh, his bald head and low eyebrows giving him an ogre like appearance. The bikers dismounted, and the truck driver reached into the back of the truck, handing them all baseball bats.

"I've seen enough. Stay here." Rexell grunted.

"Wait, you can't be going down there? You're outnumbered."

"So?" Rexell said, keeping a close eye on the group down the hill.

"They have weapons. You don't."

"Did you even read my file, Pertwee?" Rexell asked as he took off his leather jacket, exposing his muscled arms.

"Yes, of course, but-"

"Then you know what's about to go down. Now stay here, and for the love of god, shut up."

Rexell slid down the embankment, going slowly. Magnum followed, half crawling on his belly, keeping low and following his master.

Despite his desire (and orders) to keep Rexell under control, Pertwee couldn't help but be curious as to what he was about to do. More than that, he was curious to see just how much of the legends surrounding him and his exploits were true.

III

The ogrish man from the truck was called Demato. The youngest of four brothers, all of which had gone bad pretty much from the moment they could walk, he had fallen into a life of crime just as easily as a fish knows how to swim. At almost six feet seven inches and weighing in at almost four hundred and fifty pounds, he had a mean streak which was legendary in the criminal underworld. Graduating from muggings when he was a youth to burglaries and eventually armed robbery, Demato was no stranger to the criminal life. His massive forearms were adorned with self-penned prison tattoos. He squinted up at the sun, the back of his shirt already drenched in sweat. As an afterthought, he leaned back into the cab and grabbed his cap from the dashboard and put it on. He looked at Charlie and his two friends, Peter, and Alex, knowing he didn't have to say anything to them. He could see they were already deathly afraid of him and would do anything he told them.

"Remember," he said, his voice a low rumble. "Nobody does anything until I do it first. You're there for intimidation. I'll do all the talking."

"Who is this guy anyway?" Charlie said, looking over Demato's shoulder to the motorhome.

"Just some son of a bitch who owes me. We ain't leaving here without getting what we deserve."

Demato stepped towards the motorhome, his shadow thick and black against the sand, elongated as it stretched far ahead of him. At his back, Charlie and his friends waited, baseball bats thrown over shoulders, arrogant sneers on their faces.

"I know you're in there Spike," Demato said, looking for any sign of movement in the otherwise silent motorhome. "You and me got business."

He waited, letting his voice roll across the hills.

"Don't make this hard on yourself. You owe me. Five thousand. Three for the cocaine you stole from my boys here, and two for the inconvenience to my customers."

Demato waited, staring at the dusty windows.

"If you make me send my boys in there to bring you out, that's gonna cost you an extra thousand. Don't make this hard on yourself."

Demato reached into the cab of his van, pulling out the shotgun which was nestled on the seat. "I won't ask you again, Spike."

"You don't wanna do that big man."

Demato and his crew turned, watching Rexell as he walked towards them, afraid of neither men nor the weapons they carried.

"Who the hell are you?" Demato said.

"That's him," Charlie said, unsure if he was angry or afraid. "That's the guy from the diner."

"Really?" Demato said, sneering at Rexell and walking to meet him. "This is the guy that ushered you out of the meet at the diner?"

"Yeah," Charlie said, keeping a cautious eye on Rexell. "That's the son of a bitch."

"You know," Demato said, swinging the gun over his shoulder. "My associates were in that diner to conduct a business transaction. You ruined that. In turn, you cost me money."

Rexell looked Demato in the eye, showing no fear. "They were acting like assholes."

"They work for me," Demato grunted.

"I see," Rexell said as the others closed around him in a rough circle. "If they're the assholes, I guess that makes you the shit."

Demato grinned, showing the gap where his front teeth should be. "You have no idea who I am, do you?"

Rexell sighed and cracked his knuckles. "I could say the same thing to you, big man."

"You've got guts. I'll give you that." Demato said, a little wave of uncertainty crossing his face. "You can count, though, right? You see the numbers are against you here?"

"Maybe I'm dumb," Rexell replied, keeping his eyes focussed on Demato, "Or maybe I'm just confident I can put all four of your sorry asses down before you can do anything about it."

"You have guts," Demato said.

"So you said," Rexell grunted in reply. "Now are we gonna do this or are you assholes gonna stand around talking the talk."

They looked at Demato, waiting for the go ahead. He nodded, and they came for him. Just as Rexell expected, they were sloppy and wild. Charlie came first, swinging the baseball bat with little finesse, his face screwed up and more afraid than aggressive. Rexell sidestepped his lunge, slamming an open palm into his throat, using his own momentum to make the blow devastating, sending Charlie to the ground, gasping for air. Rexell could sense Alex at his back and acted instinctively, jabbing an elbow behind him. A crunch of bone on bone as elbow met teeth, the latter shattering in a bloody explosion. Alex went down, clutching his face and rolling on the ground as a wet, high pitched scream came from inside him.

Rexell looked at Peter, who still hadn't moved. He was afraid, and for a moment, Rexell thought he wouldn't try to attack, but it seemed Peter was even more afraid of Demato, and inched forward, baseball bat held at his shoulder as if he were stepping out for the first game of a new season.

"You sure you wanna do this, kid?" Rexell said, circling out of reach of the bat.

Peter looked at Demato, who glared back at him. "What the hell are you waiting for, take him down!"

Peter charged, and like the rest, he was inexperienced, all talk and nothing to back it up. He swung the bat towards Rexell, who threw a kick to meet it, knocking it out of Peter's hands. Before he could react, Rexell was on him. Grabbing him by the jacket and delivering a head butt, Peter's nose shattering in spectacular fashion. Rexell tossed him to the ground, leaving him to roll around next to Alex, and then turned his attention towards Demato. Before he could make a move, Charlie was back on him, landing a punch on Rexell's cheek.

He shook it off, the sting igniting his anger. He spun and threw out a kick, driving from the midsection, throwing the limb with venom. It caught Charlie unaware; Rexell's heavy boot catching him in the chest, the sound of Charlie's ribs breaking was incredibly crisp and clear. This time, Charlie went down and stayed there, wheezing and clutching his chest. Rexell turned towards Demato just in time to see the shotgun swinging towards him. He dived instinctively to his right just a split second before the blast from Demato's weapon kicked up a huge gout of earth. Rexell rolled into the dive and came up running, angling back towards Demato. Ten years earlier, he would have closed the distance with ease, but time spent in prison had made him lose a little pace, and he knew he wouldn't avoid the second shot. He knew Demato could see it too, his fat, greasy face flashing its toothless grin as he pointed the twin barrels directly at Rexell. He waited for it, for his insides to be ripped apart from the shot, it was then that Magnum attacked, leaping at Demato's arm, snarling and whipping his head back and forth as the shot intended for Rexell was fired harmlessly into the ground. The split second distraction was all he needed. He charged at Demato, swinging a fist at his face. The impact was spectacular, the connection good. Demato's head snapped back as he dropped the gun on the floor. Rexell hooked his boot under the gun and flicked it to safety as he waited for Demato to fall. Except Demato didn't fall. He turned back to Rexell, giving a bloody smile, then head-butted him. Rexell went down, white spots dancing in his vision. Demato swung his arm, Magnum and all towards his truck, slamming the Alsatian against it. The dog refused to let go, growling low in its throat as it continued to savage Demato's arm. He swung again, Magnum's body crashing into the bodywork hard enough to make him let go. This time, the dog fell to the dirt with a whimper.

"Back, Magnum," Rexell said as he got to his feet. The dog complied, retreating to a safe distance, face and teeth wet with blood as it watched its master and Demato circle each other. It was rare that Rexell was overmatched, but in this case, he was facing both a height and weight disadvantage. Demato threw a sloppy punch, which Rexell easily avoided. Another came at him, cutting the air inches from his face. He waited for his opportunity, for the right time to strike. Demato punched again, this time, Rexell ducked and stepped forward. He grabbed Demato's wrist with his right hand and brought his elbow down on his forearm with the left.

The snap of a broken bone was followed by the infuriated roar of agony. Rexell wasn't done, he swung a kick, one delivered with the same amount of fury he had dropped Charlie with, this time to Demato's crotch. Even as big as he was, he went to his knees, a whine which seemed too high-pitched to come from a brute as big as he was. Rexell grabbed him around the throat, hoping to say something witty or funny to end their little dispute, but again, it wasn't over, and Demato lurched, biting at Rexell, falling on top of him. Pinned under Demato's weight, he struggled to defend himself. Demato clawed and scratched, furious and red faced. Cody grabbed at the dirt, looking for anything that might help him. His hand found something. Smooth and warm. A rock. He grabbed it and swung it at Demato, connecting with the back of his skull, giving him the time he needed to get out from under his stinking mass. Still holding the rock, he climbed on Dematos massive chest and reared back to hit him.

"Stop!"

Rexell looked up, breathing heavily. Charlie had the shotgun trained on Magnum, who was still watching, waiting for Cody to give his next instruction. "Get up off him or I swear, I'll shoot it," Charlie wheezed, cheeks red, wincing from the pain of his shattered ribs.

"You should have stayed on the ground, kid," Rexell said as he stood, brushing dirt from his jeans.

"Just stay there and don't move, or I swear I'll..."

"What?" Rexell said as he walked towards Charlie. "What will you do?"

"I swear, man...."

"You don't have the guts," Rexell said, picking up his pace.

"I warned you, this is all on you, I-"

"Magnum."

It was all Rexell had to say. The dog leapt, biting and snapping, ravaging Charlie's face as he kicked and screamed on the floor. Rexell picked up the gun, casually walking back towards Demato, who was still moaning on the ground. Rexell put a boot on Demato's chest and pointed the gun at his face.

"Now I'd tell you, fat boy, not to come around here again bothering my friend, but frankly, I don't think you have the brains to pay attention. That leaves me in a bit of a dilemma."

"Fuck you, I'll kill you, I swear to God I'll kill you..." Demato said, eyes wild.

"That's what I thought you might say," Rexell said, sighing. He glanced over to Magnum who was standing beside Charlie, who was moaning on the floor, his face a bloody pulp. He turned back to Demato. "Now what would you do if you were me? I'd bet if I were lying there on the floor and you were pointing this gun at my face, there would be a good chance my brains would be splashed all over the desert by now."

"Yeah, I'd enjoy it too. If you're gonna do it, just do it."

"No, you don't get off that easy, fat boy. You and your bullying friends need to learn. Old Charlie over there, I'm pretty sure he won't forget today. I bet he'll remember it every time he looks in the mirror. Same goes for his friends there, cowering on the floor so I don't hurt them anymore. They look to have learned their lesson. That just leaves you. How can I make you remember me and Magnum here?"

Demato said nothing, he simply stared, defiant and goading, but afraid. Rexell could see that much.

"Magnum, over here," Rexell said.

He waited until the dog padded over, standing beside his master. "See, a long time ago, back before fate brought me here, I was a bounty hunter. I'd go out and find people like you, people like Charlie, and I'd bring them to justice. Sometimes, they would come quiet, and do as I said. Others, like you, were full of anger, sure you would come back for revenge just as soon as you got the chance. Those people, your kind of people are dangerous. Those are the kind of people I used to give an extra reminder to, just something to know that Magnum and I are still out there."

Rexell put his foot on Demato's forearm, pressing it into the dirt. "In the end, it got me into trouble and made it so that people were out there looking for me. Funny thing is, for each one of them they sent to bring me in, I did the same thing to them. Left my mark. My calling card. Funny how I became one of those people I was so determined to clean up. See, you and me, we're not too different. It's just that I'm good, and you are just a lazy, fat slob bully. Just remember the way this could have gone. This will hurt, there's no denying that, but at least you'll live through it. In a week or a month from now, when you're feeling brave and decide you want to come after me? I want you to think about the pain I'm about to cause you. The reminder. I'll leave you with two." He glanced at Demato's hand as he said it. "A reminder. The index finger to remind you of me, the thumb to remind you of Magnum sitting by my side."

"You think I'm scared of you? I'll kill you. I'll never stop, never I'll-"

"Magnum, take three," Rexell said.

The dog attacked, chewing and biting, shredding and tearing, removing Demato's fingers one at a time until just thumb and forefinger remained. When it was done, Rexell stepped back, looking at his handiwork. He finally glanced down at Demato. The aggression and fight had gone out of him now. He lay in the dirt, clutching his ravaged hand to his chest.

"We're done here," Rexell said. "Get going, now. I don't want to see you here again."

Alex and Peter scrambled towards Charlie, half dragging him to the truck, his face barely recognizable behind the blood mask he wore.

"What about Charlie's bike?" Peter asked, glancing at the motorcycle.

"That stays here. Payment for inconveniencing me and harassing my friend."

Demato opened his mouth, then closed it, cheeks red with fury. Rexell watched him, daring him to say something. Instead, he got up as best he could, pulling himself up the side of the pickup and leaving a bloody smear on the bodywork. He reached to pick up his chewed up fingers with his good hand, when Rexell stepped on it, crushing it into the dirt.

"No, fat boy. Leave those. They belong to me now. I earned them."

Demato glared but said nothing. Rexell lifted his foot and let him go, watching as he carefully got into the cab, glancing over at the bloodied Charlie in the passenger seat. Alex and Peter were already on their bikes, firing them up and snaking away from the trailer. Demato tried to turn the key in the ignition, his hand shaking. Once. Twice. He got it on the third attempt, gunning the engine. He glared at Rexell, a little of the fire and anger back in him now that he knew he was going to live.

"This isn't over," Demato grunted. "Not by a long shot."

Rexell grinned. "Yeah, they all say that. Go on, fat boy. Get the hell out of here. Get Charlie to a hospital. Yourself too."

Demato revved the engine, desperate to say or do something but not quite able to commit to doing either. Instead, he accelerated away, leaving a cloud of dust in his wake. Rexell watched them go, and then looked at Magnum, scratching him behind the ear.

"Come on then Mag, let's go find uncle Spike."

Magnum trotted forward as Rexell followed him towards the trailer.

IV

Rexell pushed open the door, poking his head into the dusty trailer. Beer bottles and clutter covered every surface, and Rexell wrinkled his nose at the slightly musty, sweaty smell.

Magnum whined and snorted, standing ready to follow Rexell inside.

"Stay here, Mag," He whispered, quietly stepping inside and gently closing the door.

He stood, listening for any sign of his friend. He looked down the length of the camper. Tiny, dirty kitchen, the sink full of dirty dishes. Beyond, a cramped seating area piled high with dirty clothes. Three doors were further down the camper. He suspected one was a bathroom, the other a bedroom. The third he had no idea. He walked slowly, pausing by the sink to grab the knife sitting by its side, some congealed substance clinging to it which looked like some kind of pizza. He inched forward, approaching the first door. It was open, and he could see it was a bathroom, the toilet in serious need of a clean. He moved on. To his right, the second door was closed, as was the one straight ahead. Rexell inched open the first door, exhaling when he saw that it was a pantry. It was filled with all manner of tins and packages of foods. Below it, a small grubby fridge hummed quietly.

A bump. A stealthy thud from behind the door he hadn't checked out yet. He adjusted his grip on the knife, putting a cautious hand on the door handle. He considered the slow approach, then decided it wasn't really his style. Instead, he took a step back and kicked the door, the cheap wood splintering.

A roar of gunfire reverberated around the confines of the camper, causing Rexell to duck back as the doorframe exploded in a shower of wood splinters.

Rexell turned, ready to throw the knife, and then stopped.

"Spike?"

"Rex?"

The two men stared at each other, Rexell shaking his head. Spike sat in his bed, sheets pulled around his middle. He was around forty, his hair black but thinning on top. His cheeks were lined with stubble, and his eyes were cold. In his prime, he was the kind of men women would do anything for. Now, however, his looks were starting to go, and it was only his bad boy attitude that kept him in their favour. Beside him, a woman, slim and voluptuous and half his age sat beside him, horrified and giving Rexell a good view of her impressive and seemingly gravity oblivious chest.

"What the hell are you doing, Spike?" Rexell said, lowering the weapon.

"I thought you were one of Demato's people coming in to get me."

"You couldn't have come out?" Rexell said, shaking his head.

"Candy and I were busy if you know what I'm saying. No way I was breaking off just to go deal with that asshole."

"That asshole would have killed you if I hadn't shown up."

"You underestimate me, Rex," Spike said with a grin. He pulled the covers off, showing the rest of Candy's body and the pump action shotgun she was holding under the sheets.

"Impressive. Rexell said. "Either way, I doubt he'll be back. He says you owe him money."

"I do. Him and every other asshole between here and Vegas."

"Still gambling I take it?"

"Every day."

"Winning?"

"Not so much," Spike said with a wink. "I pretty much break even. Hey, there's beer in the fridge if you want one."

"No thanks, I'm good."

"Still not drinking, huh?"

Rexell said nothing. Spike shrugged.

"Ah well, that's up to you. Anyway, what are you doing here? Last I heard you were inside. Alcatraz if word on the street is right."

"I was."

"And they just let you out?" Spoke said eyebrows raised.

"Not exactly. It's... complicated."

"I take it you came here to get Tina?" Spike said.

"Yeah, weapons too if you can help me out."

"Of course, you know you're always welcome here. What say you give me five minutes to get dressed and I'll meet you out front?"

"Yeah, no problem."

Candy leaned over and whispered in Spike's ear.

"Uhh, actually, can you make it ten? I've got something to finish here first if you know what I'm saying."

"Some things never change, huh Spike?" Rexell replied, unable to hide his smile.

V

The ten minutes became twenty, and by the time Spike appeared outside, bare-chested, drinking a beer and dressed in grubby jeans and slippers, Pertwee had arrived and was standing with Rexell as Magnum chewed on a monstrous beef bone in the shade of the trailer. Spike looked Pertwee up and down and then turned to Rexell.

"Who's the suit?"

"He's with me," Rexell replied.

"I'm a friend." Pertwee cut in.

"Bullshit you are. You're either police or government. Either way, it makes me uncomfortable." Spike replied.

"It's fine, he understands the rules. This is off the books, Spike. Don't worry about it."

"Come on Rex, you know I didn't last this long in my business without being cautious. I don't want anyone coming sniffing around here after you're done with whatever the hell you're doing out here."

"Look," Pertwee said, holding up his palms. "I can assure you, nothing untoward will happen to you. I'm here to escort Mr Rexell. That's all."

Spike looked at Pertwee, holding his gaze until the government official looked away. "Well, I don't know much about that, but I do know Rex is my friend, and if he says it's cool, then it's cool."

"Alright," Pertwee said. "To tell you the truth, I don't even know why we came out here."

"The man came back for his dog. I've been looking after him."

"That's not all though is it?" Pertwee asked.

Rexell and Spike glanced at each other. "No," they said at the same time.

"You sure you want to let him see, Rex?"

"No choice, I can't get rid of him even if I wanted to."

"Alright, but remember, you asked for this," Spike said. He walked to the rear of the red truck and dug his hands into the soft, dry sand there. He stood, pulling with him a chain. He dragged it out of the sand and hooked it on to the tow bar on the rear of the truck, then walked to the cab, staring at Pertwee as he climbed in. The engine sounded sick but eventually sputtered to life. The truck rolled forward, pulling the chain, which in turn pulled open a cover hidden under the sand, a dark maw dug into the earth with a steel ramp leading down. Spike put the vehicle into park and climbed out of the truck.

"Come on then, let's go take a look," He said, leading the way down the ramp. Rexell and Magnum followed, Pertwee, bringing up the rear. It was noticeably cooler as they descended, and the air had a musty, oily smell. Spike went to the wall and flicked a switch, a series of lights flickering on to show them the room.

It was a concrete bunker approximately thirty feet square. Each wall was lined with racks containing all manner of weapons. Rifles and shotguns, rocket launchers and grenades. Boxes filled with land mines and dynamite. Pertwee stared, eyes wide.

"This is so illegal," he muttered, voice echoing around the cavernous space.

"Why do you think I was worried about bringing you here?"

"That her?" Rexell said, nodding to the tarpaulin covered object in the middle of the room.

"Yeah, that's her," Spike replied.

Rexell walked to the green canvas tarp, throwing it back in a cloud of dust.

"I tucked her in, just like you asked," Spike said.

The car was a 1957 GT Shelby 500, its bodywork a deep and immaculate red despite being in its underground tomb. Low and sleek, the car's chrome grille glittered in the dim overhead lighting. "There she is," Rexell said, running a hand across the hood. He opened the door and ducked inside, breathing in the smell.

"Nice car," Pertwee said, still staring at the weapons. "Dare I ask if this is legal too?"

"If you mean do I own it, yes I do," Rexell said, climbing in behind the wheel, re-familiarizing himself with the car. "Also had some modifications done. Upgraded the engine, reinforced the bodywork."

"Dare I ask why?" Pertwee said.

"I wouldn't. Less you know the better."

"For once I think I agree. So what now?"

Rexell climbed out of the car and turned to spike. "I need weapons."

"Small arms?"

"No," Rexell shook his head. "I need powerful, high-end stuff."

"What are you doing, taking down an elephant?"

"Something like that," Rexell grumbled. "What have you got for me?"

"I can load you up with a rocket launcher. Oh, wait, I have just the thing."

Spike hurried across the room, dragging a crate from under one of the shelves. "Come take a look," he called over his shoulder.

Rexell and Pertwee followed, looking inside the straw covered wooden box. "I just got these in last week," Spike said, grinning.

Pertwee took one of the dull steel grenades out of the box, turning it over and over in his hands. "These are Russian," He said, staring at Spike.

"I know."

"How the hell did you get these?"

"Relax, a friend of mine got his hands on some stuff and offloaded them to me."

"Do you know the trouble you'll be in if you get caught with these?" Pertwee said.

"I think you're more worried about the trouble you'll be in by the look on your face."

"You don't understand. Ever since Stalin died we-"

"Look, I know things are tense between us and them right now." Spike cut in. "But I'm also very careful when it comes to my business. For the record, these grenades are better than our U.S counterparts. Bigger blast radius, more bang for the buck."

"I'll take them," Rexell said. "What else?"

"Do you need any hand to hand weapons? Just got some new knives. Really, really good quality stuff."

"Yeah, I'll take one. Also, I'll need ammo and maybe a shotgun."

"Done."

"Hey, uh, Spike. I don't have any money to cover all this now." Rexell said.

Spike nodded and closed the lid of the box of Russian grenades. "Alright, then let's work something out."

"You know I'm good for it, but I can't get to my cash yet. Not until I do this job."

"Look, Rex, I trust you like a brother. Anyone else would be out of here with my foot up their ass, but you've always been good to me, so I'll cut you a deal. You pay me when you can, that's fine. But I'll need a deposit."

"I already told you, I don't have any money. Not to cover this. Not yet."

"Let me finish," Spike said, turning and sitting on the lip of the crate. "Like I said, you pay me later, plus a little extra for my inconvenience. In the meantime, as far as a deposit goes....I'm hungry and I could use something to eat. You buy me breakfast, and you can settle the rest later."

Rexell shook Spike's hand, then the two men embraced. "I owe you one, Spike."

"Don't you always, you son of a bitch," Spike grinned. "Now let's get out of here, I'm hungry."

CHAPTER SIX

REXELL WONDERED IF THEY would remember him when he went back to the diner. That question was answered by the way all eyes fell on them as they walked through the door. Spike was finishing his breakfast, bacon and eggs washed down with gallons of coffee. Rexell had hoped to see Marion again, but she was busy when they got there, flitting between customers. She glanced in his direction as he entered, and then looked away. Rexell sat at a booth, cradling his coffee and waiting to see what Spike would say.

"So what were you in for? Alcatraz I mean," Spike said as he swallowed more bacon.

"I thought you'd heard about it on the grapevine."

"I knew they were looking for you for that whole bounty hunting gig. Word was you went into business for yourself, chopping off fingers."

"Yeah," Rexell said, sipping his coffee and returning the gaze of an old man who was watching him from across the room, causing him to put his head back behind his newspaper.

"What I also heard was that you gave yourself up." Spike looked at him, eyebrows raised.

"I didn't hear a question," Rexel said.

"Is it true?"

Rexell sighed and folded his hands on the table, cradling his cup. "If you're asking if it's true I gave myself up, then yeah, I did."

"That's not like you, Rex. Why would you do that?"

Rexell leaned forward, staring at his friend. "I've known you for a long time, Spike. Why don't you just ask me what I know you really want to talk to me about?"

Spike chewed his food and set his fork down, then took a sip of his coffee. "Alright, I will. I heard a rumour, something that somehow got legs and became fact. Hell, you know how these things work. Chinese whispers."

"Yeah, I know. What did you hear?"

Spike sighed, wiping his mouth on a napkin then tossing it on his plate.

"I heard that during the whole bounty hunting thing, you disappeared, went to lay low in Mexico."

Spike waited for some kind of confirmation but was met only with the steely gaze of Rexell. He went on. "I heard you met a girl there. Settled down, started a family. This was all talk, you understand. A guy like you doesn't just disappear without people wondering where you are, you know? Anyways, I heard you were out of the game. Done, retired. The great Cody Rexell finally tamed by a woman, and then..." He swallowed and looked at his empty, grease-streaked plate, then at his empty coffee cup.

"Go on. I want to hear the rest of it."

"I heard – and again, this is just a rumour Rex – that when you were there, your woman and kid were walking home at night. Some say it was a birthday party, some say it was just from picking up groceries. Anyway, the story went that they were walking down the side of the road when this drunk comes out of nowhere. Way over the limit, weaving all over the place. He didn't even see them as he came round the bend on the wrong side of the road. Word is neither of them stood a chance. They say you couldn't handle it, started drinking, getting involved with the gangs down there. They say they put a bounty on your head, they called you, 'El Gran Diablo Blanco'. The Great White Devil. After that, it all went quiet. Just rumours and legends. Sightings that may or may not have been you. Next thing I hear is that you gave yourself up and were sent to Alcatraz. Four years later you come walking into my trailer out of the blue this morning. You have to see why I'm curious. So you tell me, is that how it happened?"

Rexell sipped his drink, staring over the top of Spike's head, recalling long hidden memories.

"Almost," he said, his voice quiet, almost a mumble. Pertwee also looked on. This was the first time he had seen Rexell be anything but loud and brash since they had met.

"It seems you have part of the truth and part bullshit. That's not your fault, though. If you want the truth, I think you better hear it from me." Rexell set his cup down, and then looked at Spike and Pertwee. "After the whole bounty hunter thing got out of hand, things got too hot here. I had police looking for me which was bad enough, but I also had the gangs. Mobsters looking to make a name for themselves and kill me to get their reward. I had safe houses of course. Friends, people like you, Spike. People who would always be there to help me. Thing is, the gangs and the cops knew about them too. They started pressuring them, watching them, threatening them. Two good friends of mine ended up in prison. Another three were taken by the gangs and murdered as a message. That's when I knew it was time to get away and keep my profile low."

"And that's when you went to Mexico?" Pertwee said. Rexell nodded.

"Yeah. It was the one place I knew I could go and get a fresh start. Lay low, keep my head from getting blown off. There's nothing like being a wanted man, Pertwee. Nothing worse than worrying that every sound you hear, every person you see on the street is out to get you. I had no ties, nothing to keep me here, so I went to Mexico. I asked a friend to take my car and Magnum to Spike and ask him to look after both."

"I remember that Jonny Goodman brought them in."

"Yeah. It wasn't safe for me to come and do it myself. Not with them watching. Anyway, so I went to Mexico, and it was like a breath of fresh air. I learned to relax. I learned to live again."

"What about the girl? Was she real?" Spike asked.

Rexell nodded, staring out of the window at the parking lot.

"Her name was Michelle. Local girl, beautiful eyes. I met her in a bar there, and the two of us just hit it off. It was like we had always known each other, you know? Anyways, we got together, and I moved her into my place. A year goes by and she has a kid. A boy." He smiled, but it was without humour. "He looked like me. Same eyes, same nose. Her mouth and skin colour. She wanted to call him after me, but I wasn't keen on that. I didn't want any kid of mine to be associated with what I'd done, so she settled on Jose. Anyway, things are starting to get strained. I'm not cut out to be a father, and after the life I'd been used to living, I couldn't adjust. We started to fight. At first every other week, but then every day. I didn't know it then, but I think I've figured it out since. I was trying to push her away. I was trying to alienate myself."

"You don't need to talk about this Rex, not if you don't want to," Spike said.

"It's alright. It's better you know the truth. Anyways, this one day we had a huge fight. Screaming and shouting her scratching, me just trying to hold her back, kid screaming in the background. She storms out of the house, taking Jose with her. She said she was going to her mother's for a few days."

"That's when it happened? When the drunk hit her?"

Rexell nodded. "Yeah, it was. That son of a bitch cut them down and didn't even know anything about it until he had sobered up enough to understand." Rexell lowered his head, staring at his coffee cup.

"It was you, wasn't it?" Pertwee asked. "You were driving the car."

Rexell nodded. "Thing is I wasn't even chasing after them to say sorry. I was going after them to carry on the argument, to drive home my point. I'd been drinking vodka and beer, and whatever else I could lay my hands on. I shouldn't have been driving. Anyway, I collected them on the side of the road and ran the car into a ditch. By the time I'd sobered up, they had already been taken away in an ambulance and I was in the back of a police car waiting to be questioned. I escaped, and then I went into this... cycle. I wanted to die. I was getting into the faces of the gangs, trying to goad them into killing me. Trying to make them put me out of my misery. How could I know my craziness would make them scared of me?"

"Then you gave yourself up?" Pertwee asked.

"Not straight away. See by then, the self-pity had gone and been replaced by anger. Frustration. I lashed out at the gangs, and let me tell you, in Mexico, they don't screw around. Here, they might rough you up, or maybe even stab you. Over there, they don't think twice about cutting off your head or burning you alive. One by one, gang by gang, I killed them. Leaving my mark, cutting off the fingers on the right hand apart from index and thumb. I wanted them to know it was me, you know? I wanted them to be able to find me. I wanted them to kill me. By then, the police here as well as there were onto me, and I was back where I started. At that point, running didn't feel like something I was willing or able to do anymore. I gave myself up. I didn't care what happened to me."

Pertwee cleared his throat, then slid out of the booth. "I uh, I'll let the two of you talk for a while. I'll be outside" He made his exit, leaving the two friends behind.

"Jesus," Spike said. "I wouldn't have brought it up if I'd known it was so bad. Are you coping okay now?"

Rexell shrugged. "I've learned to live with it. It's my burden to bear."

"No, it's not. I'm your friend. Whatever you want, I'm here for you."

Rexell grinned. "Not much a man can say to ease the pain for someone who is responsible for killing his own kid. I sometimes dream about them, about running them down. That's the strange thing. I always see it in my dreams, but don't know if that's how it went down or if it's just my brain painting a picture of what it thinks happened. That bothers me that I was too out of it to remember doing it."

Spike exhaled and looked out of the window, not sure what to say. Rexell looked past him, lost in the pain of his memories. "Anyway," he said eventually, forcing a strained smile. "That's in the past. And I don't want to bore you with it anymore."

"I'm not bored by it, Rex. I'm just surprised. I've never seen this side of you before. You've changed."

"Yeah, well, people do. I just wish I knew what the hell I was supposed to do with my life now."

Pertwee hurried back into the diner, eyes flicking nervously from Rexell to Spike. "We have to go, now."

"What's the rush?" Rexell said.

"Something's happened. An...incident." Pertwee said.

"Spit it out, Pertwee."

Pertwee glanced at Spike. "I can't say it in front of him. You know that."

"I already know about your giant worm," Spike cut in. "He already told me."

"That's classified information," Pertwee hissed under his breath.

"Not anymore," Rexell said, sliding out of the booth. "What's the big news?"

"We need to get out of here now and get to Montana," Pertwee said as he led them out of the diner and towards his car. "I've made arrangements for a cargo plane to pick us up at the airport since you insisted on taking your car."

"I've been apart from her for too long. Now, do you want to tell me what this is about?"

Pertwee spun to face Rexell, his brow furrowed, dark anger in his eyes. "I told you we couldn't afford to delay and now this has happened."

"What?" Rexell asked."

"The creature. It's....made an attack."

"Where?" Rexell asked.

II

Rexell walked towards the door to the diner, brow furrowed as he took in all that Pertwee had said. Marion approached him as he left. Her eyes said she wanted to speak, but she couldn't find any words.

"How are you doing?" Rexell asked.

"I'm fine," she said, staring at the floor. He could see the marks on her arms even though she tried to hide them.

"Who did that?"

"It was nothing."

"Was it our friends from the other day?"

She looked at him then, and he could see why she was so reluctant to meet his gaze. She was afraid. "They came to my house. Threatened me. Asked me all sorts of questions about you."

"When was this?"

"A couple of days ago. Said you owed them for what you did to them, whatever that means."

"Yeah, well, since then those guys and me have had more words. I doubt they'll bother you again."

"What happened to them?"

"Less you know the better."

Pertwee banged on the door, pointing at his watch. "Look, I gotta go. Things to do."

"I'm scared they'll come back. Those guys are trouble. What if they do something to me because they can't get to you?"

He hadn't considered that particular possibility. There was every chance that she was right. "Alright, here's what we're gonna do."

III

Pertwee fidgeted by his car, nervously checking his watch. Rexell exited the diner, Marion following. "What's this?"

She's coming with us."

"No, absolutely not. Too many civilians have already got themselves involved in this."

Rexell stopped, standing in front of Pertwee. "She's in trouble and it's my fault."

"That's not our problem. What kind of trouble could she possibly be in that involves you?"

"Remember those guys from the trailer? It seems they have developed a bit of an interest in me and are trying to take it out on her. Until I can find the time to have words, she's staying with us for protection."

"What if I say no?" Pertwee said, flicking his jacket open to show his gun holster.

Rexell grinned and whistled through his teeth. Magnum stuck his head out of the driver's side door of Rexell's vehicle, muscles bunched as he growled and drooled into the floor. "Your call, Pertwee," Rexell said. "If you want me to fix this problem, we do it my way. You know that."

Pertwee was ready to explode, but couldn't say anything. He was under instruction to do whatever Rexell saw fit. "Fine, let's just get on with it."

"Where are we going?" Marion asked.

"Montana," Rexell said as he shooed Magnum back and got into his car.

CHAPTER SEVEN
West Yellowstone Elementary School
Montana

THE EARTHQUAKE HAD ALREADY done a small amount damage to West Yellowstone Elementary School. The tremors had opened up a long crack in the east wall and destroyed a stone monument which had stood outside for some time. Workmen buzzed around and worked on repairing the damage as lessons went on, the staff at the school determined that the event would have as little disruption as possible to the education of its students. Al Greenwood stood and stared at the collapsed birch entryway, then at his two men that had come with him to help clean up the damage. The city wanted everything dealt with as swiftly as possible, and although Al was happy to help, he was already exhausted, cranky and in need of sleep. He waved the dump truck in, beckoning it toward him as it reversed carefully onto the grass outside the school, unaware that in doing so, the vibrations of the vehicle had reverberated into the tunnel hollowed out fifteen feet below the surface, and had alerted something that there was an encroachment onto its territory.

II

At almost sixty feet in length and weighing close to three tons, the creature moved through the earth, burrowing with ease. Much like a common earthworm, the creature possessed two sets of muscles under its three-inch thick skin. The first is a layer of circular muscles running around the circumference of the creature's body. Underneath, a thicker layer of longitudinal muscles stretches the length of the creature's body. As the circular muscles contract, the creature compresses, shrinking around the middle. As the longitudinal muscles then contract the worm becomes shorter and fatter, enabling it to move through the earth. In addition, each ringed segment on the creature's body has its own set of circular and longitudinal muscles, along with four pairs of setae, a collection of thick, stiff hairs which act as both protection and as a means to cling to its surrounding burrow so that it can dig and move comfortably in any direction. The vibrations coming from the school both aggravated and enticed it, and unsure if it was prey or predator, the worm had cut towards the school, driven by instinct to either fight or feed.

III

Al barked orders, making sure the men knew he was in charge. He was getting a headache, and the very last thing he'd wanted was to have a major clean-up operation to look after. Anxious school children stood outside the school, pointing and whispering, enjoying the unexpected reprieve from lessons. The rumble was subtle at first, a distant vibration which made the loose stones on the rubble pile roll to the sidewalk.

"Shut that engine off," Al snapped, enjoying the power of being in authority. Silence filled the air, and even the birds had stopped singing. Al tilted his head, narrowing his eyes as he listened as if it would help him to isolate what the rumble was. He had decided it was likely an aftershock and was about to tell those watching to take cover when the ground sank beneath him. He stumbled and fell as the worm breached, clamping its ring of circular serrated teeth around his leg and severing it with ease. Al screamed, the pain, unlike anything he had ever experienced before. Blood from his severed arteries sprayed across the sun-drenched concrete, as those watching went into a panic, unaware that the vibrations of their running feet were further stimulus for the worm. It went under again, burrowing through the earth at speed, homing in on the people who were unaware of its presence. It breached again under an old couple who were desperately trying to flee, moving as quickly as they could with the aid of their walking sticks. The worm took the man first, coming up behind and taking the man's feet, its rows of concentric circular teeth flexing as they pulled the man further into its stomach, the sound of his bones breaking lost in the screams of the citizens.

A police car arrived, then, seeing the huge creature in the road, swerved, crashing into a storefront, sending the already frightened people into even more of a frenzy. Officer Dwayne Hicks climbed out of the car, staring at the creature which had now almost entirely devoured the old man. Hicks pulled his revolver and fired at the creature, his bullets landing but seemingly doing nothing but further aggravating it. He had seen enough. It was way more than he could handle. He leaned back into the car and grabbed the radio. "We need some help here right now and I don't just mean other officers. Get the army down here if you have to. We need to seal this town off. There's a.... look just do it. I can't control this crowd by myself."

IV

An hour passed, and the town had started to resemble a war zone. It had been sealed off, green army trucks arriving by the dozen and filled with men who were too proud to show they were frightened. The streets were deserted as four such soldiers inched towards the hole where the worm had first breached. They sidestepped bodies, ignored the pools of blood on the ground. They even tried to ignore the damage. Glass shattered and twinkling on the pavements under the glow of streetlights, the school, leaning to one side, the damage caused by the earthquake the most minor of its battle scars. The one thing they couldn't ignore was the hole, the burrow made by the worm as it had burst out of the ground. The four soldiers approached weapons drawn, eyes wide and alert, hearts thundering in rib cages.

Corporal James T. Anderson wrinkled his nose as they neared. "You smell that?" he whispered.

"Yeah, smells like rotten meat." One of the other soldiers replied, a young man with jet black hair and a strong jawline called David Miloy.

The group stopped, not by any command, but by collecting subconscious instinct. The wormhole was ten feet away from them, the broken asphalt around its edge laced with thick strands of translucent slime.

"What the hell is that?" Perkins said, turning to Miloy and Anderson.

"Beats me. Looks like snot or somethin'" Miloy muttered.

"Quiet, all of you." Sgt Jenkins hissed.

They did as instructed, waiting for Jenkins to make a decision. The Sgt. was in his thirties, his skin leathery and worn, making him appear closer to forty. His eyes had the perpetual droop of the proverbial puppy dog, and his black moustache sat above a humourless, pencil line of a mouth. "Alright, Miloy, on me. Perkins, approach in from the right, Anderson, the left. Keep your eyes open, and remember, don't do anything stupid. Wait for me before you make a move."

The soldiers dispersed, veering off and angling towards the hole from their instructed directions. Jenkins and Miloy approached the hole head on, trying as best they could to ignore the despicable smell coming out of it.

Jenkins arrived first and glanced at his men, men he trusted, men he had gone to war with. He saw the same fear in them that he was feeling, yet knew they wouldn't desert him, just as he wouldn't desert his duty, no matter what lay ahead.

He turned to Miloy, who was unable to hide his fear, a light sweat on his brow. "Keep your eyes open, Miloy. I'm going to lean over there and take a look."

Miloy nodded, lifting his gun into firing position, nestling it against his shoulder. Jenkins put a foot on the edge of the hole, wincing as dirt fell back into the hole. He peered over, waiting for his eyes to adjust to the gloom. When they did, he wasn't entirely sure at first what it was they were seeing. Only when his brain managed to put the pieces together, did fear truly hit him, and with it took away any ideas of proceeding further.

"Back, fall back, all of you. Back behind the barricade." Jenkins was already moving, feet crunching on concrete as he moved away from the hole.

"What is it? What did you see, Sir?" Miloy said as he followed, alarmed at the Sgt's behaviour.

Jenkins however, didn't answer. All he could think of was reaching safety, and hoping that one day he could forget what he had seen in the burrow.

CHAPTER EIGHT

BY THE FOLLOWING MORNING, there were more people on site. More police, more soldiers, most of all, more civilians, all of them craning their necks to try and get a peek beyond the barricade as they speculated what was going on.

The aggressive, throaty growl of Rexell's Shelby roused them from their boredom as he rolled towards the barricade, Marion in the back with Pertwee, Magnum in the passenger seat, head hanging out of the window and tongue lolling from his mouth. Rexell gunned the engine again, just to make sure he had everyone's attention, then switched it off and climbed out of the car, Magnum leaping out of the open window and standing beside his master, tail swishing slightly as they waited for Pertwee to get out of the car. He was dishevelled, his suit dirty, his shirt ringed with sweat. Rexell had to fight hard not to laugh.

"Why the hell did I have to squeeze into the back? Isn't that the dog's place?" Pertwee grumbled.

"Magnum rides up front."

"He's a goddamn dog." Pertwee hissed as he wiped a hand across his sweaty brow.

"True. But he's tougher than you. I trust him more. And," Rexell leaned forward, then wrinkled his nose. "Yeah, he smells better too. He rides up front. End of story."

"Very funny." Pertwee sighed and tried his best to smarten his appearance. "Alright, let's go see what we can find out. We're expected."

Rexell and Marion followed Pertwee into the crowd, who parted at the sight of such an imposing figure. "Wait here Magnum. Keep an eye on the car." Rexell said over his shoulder.

The Alsatian obeyed, retreating to the vehicle and leaping in through the open passenger side window, then poking its head out, watching his master leave.

Pertwee gave the police at the barricade his credentials, and the trio was waved through.

On the other side of the barricade, some distance from the watching crowd, a command post had been set up. Makeshift tents had been erected, and soldiers buzzed around completing tasks. Pertwee paused outside the largest of the green tents and turned to Rexell.

"Alright, here's the deal. Let me do the talking here, okay? The guy in charge can be a real tough cookie. He also isn't too happy about us coming in and treading on his toes, even less so about me bringing a convicted criminal in. Just stand still, keep quiet and try not to provoke him."

"Does he have a name?"

"Shaw. He's some kind of high end commander. He's already pissed that he's had to come out here on no sleep and be pulled from his vacation. Just play nice, okay?

"You're no fun, Pertwee."

"This isn't about fun. We have a serious incident here. The last thing I need is you getting under the skin of the locals"

Rexell nodded, half wishing he had brought Magnum along on the off chance that Shaw was as much of an asshole as Pertwee was saying. "Alright Pertwee, you do the talking. I'll behave. You have my word."

"Alright, thanks," Pertwee said, visibly relaxing.

As he followed, Rexell almost felt sorry for him for believing him.

II

Inside the tent was cool, and furnished with a desk behind which Shaw sat. He stood as they entered, giving them a look as if they had just shit on his floor.

"I wondered when you might show up," Shaw grunted, as he stood and folded his arms.

He was a big guy, well over six feet of muscle. He had a strong jawline and a short, thick neck which seemed to melt into his shoulders. His hair was sandy and cut short. He flicked his cruel blue eyes from Rexell, Pertwee, to Marion then back to Pertwee. "What is this, some kind of goddamn freak show?"

"I understand your frustration, Commander Shaw. I assure you we won't be stepping on your toes any longer than we have to."

Shaw turned to Rexell, glaring at him. Rexell stared back. "And what's with the criminal? Why is he here?"

"I'm here to do the job you can't get done," Rexell said as Pertwee winced.

"What did you say to me, son?" Shaw said, striding around his desk.

"You heard me."

"Commander. You will refer to me as Commander or Sir."

"No, I won't."

Shaw was getting red in the face. Rexell wondered if steam would come out of his ears if he continued to poke him.

"You'll show me the proper respect. I'm in charge here. Who the hell do you think you are coming in here and saying I can't do my damn job?"

Rexell grinned, stepping forward so that he was almost face to face with the commander. "I never said you couldn't do the job."

"Sounds like it to me. Or was it some other asshole who doesn't know what the hell he's talking about?"

"Maybe you should ask the president. It was him who sent me."

"Alright, everyone, please calm down." Pertwee stammered, trying to push between them. "I think we can all agree that the best way forward is to just all do our jobs. We all have orders to follow, let's just do that and we can go our separate ways."

"This is a farce. A goddamn farce." Shaw snapped as he retreated to his desk. He sat down hard and folded his hands on the table top, his gold wedding ring glittering under the artificial light. "What is it that you need?"

Pertwee adjusted his tie, the relief evident as he glared at Rexell then turned towards Shaw. "A briefing on what happened here. And access to the site."

"Access won't be a problem. The whole place has been shut down waiting for you two to arrive, although I don't have a goddamn clue why. We can handle it. This is a goddamn circus, nobody should-"

"-Commander, an update if you will? Time is precious here as I'm sure you can imagine."

Shaw was furious. The redness in his face had increased, and his jaw was clenched, cheek twitching as he glared alternately at Rexell and Pertwee. "Well, let me give you the quick version. I sent my men out to investigate the burrow in the street by the school, see if our worm was still in there when they arrived they saw something that made them turn and run."

"What did they see?" Pertwee asked.

"Took all night to get any sense out of them. Only one of the men saw it and he was hysterical for the most part until we gave him some meds to calm him down. Later in the night, he calmed enough to tell us. He said he saw a kid down there, all cocooned and wrapped in this slimy, gunky shit."

"Dead?"

"We assumed so at first, but wanted to be sure, so we sent another team out to the hole to try and retrieve it. When they got to the hole they saw the kid, half wrapped in this cocoon. It seems our worm either got bored or disturbed mid wrap, anyway, we pulled the kid out, got him back here and cut that slimy shit off him."

"He alive?" Rexell asked.

"Yeah, the kid lived. Shaken up and malnourished, but alive."

"That's something, at least," Pertwee said.

"I haven't finished yet." Shaw snapped. "So we pull out the kid and think all is well, right, or at least until we check the register of the pupils in the school. There are twenty of them unaccounted for. We're guessing this worm is using the school as a goddamn nest and has these kids wrapped up in there somewhere."

"Jesus," Pertwee said, sitting on the chair opposite Shaw. "These cocoons, are we assuming they're for....storage."

Shaw nodded. "That's our best guess. Seems our worm is prepping food for the cold months and has started with a whole class full of kids. We haven't seen it since the attack, but we can hear it alright, crashing and banging around under the school."

"Jesus, so what do we do next?"

Pertwee watched as Shaw leaned back in his chair, stared at them and smiled. "That's on you. We were told to stand down until you arrived, and now here you are. Our saviours, our knights in shining armour. I have men here who were chomping at the bit to go in there and pull these kids out and are sitting on their hands because someone in a suit decided you were the better option. Well, to that I say, go do it. Go do the job we can't and save these kids before they become this thing's supper."

Pertwee turned to Rexell. "I need to call this in. Surely you can see this is bigger than you?"

Rexell ignored him and turned to Shaw. "How far is the school?"

"Down the street. You can't miss it. Unless you have a big ass fishing rod to snag this thing, I wouldn't advise going out there." Shaw sneered, now enjoying the way things were unfolding.

"Let's get out of here," Rexell said to Pertwee.

"I agree. We need to call this in. Commander Shaw, accept my apologies I-"

"Take Marion back to the car."

"What do you mean? Surely you're not going down there?" Pertwee said.

"I want my freedom. This is the only way I see how to get it."

"It's suicide. You don't know what's in that school."

Shaw laughed, breaking both Rexell and Pertwee from their conversation. "Something funny?"

"Everything," Shaw said, leaning back in his seat and propping his booted feet up on the desk. "You have no idea what you're up against here. I almost feel sorry for you."

"Really?" Rexell said, walking towards Shaw's desk.

"Am I supposed to be scared? Intimidated? I have fifty men out there who will tear you to pieces if you even so much as-"

Rexell hit him, fist connecting with nose, sending Shaw toppling backwards onto the floor, his broken nose bleeding all over his army fatigues. The commander made no attempt to get up, instead, he stared at Rexell who glared back at him. "If any of your men want to try their luck, you know where I'll be."

Rexell strode out of the tent; Pertwee and Marion open mouthed as they watched him leave. They followed, wanting to be out of Shaw's way before he got up. Pertwee was part angry, part afraid.

"You've done it now. That's too far. I told you to let me do the talking I told you to-"

"Give it a rest, Pertwee. He had it coming. Now get back to the car."

"You can't just walk in there alone with no weapons. It's crazy."

Rexell put his fingers to his lips and whistled. "Who said I was going in there alone?"

They watched as Magnum sprinted towards them, head down, muscles bunched. He came to a stop in front of Rexell and then sat, panting and waiting for his master's instructions.

"Go wait in the car. I want to check things out."

"You need weapons. Surely you must see that?" Marion said as Pertwee nodded in agreement.

"Not yet."

"Why not?"

"Because there are kids in there."

Rexell watched as realization dawned. He turned and walked down the street, Magnum keeping pace alongside him as Pertwee and Marion retreated to the car.

II

Rexell and Magnum halted outside the school. The silence was total apart from Magnum's panted breath. A light breeze ruffled Rexell's hair, and he wrinkled his nose. "That you, Magnum?"

The dog looked at him, then turned away, snorting down its nose.

"Guess not," Rexell muttered. "Well, we better go take a look."

Rexell walked to the entrance to the school, pausing by the door. He glanced at Magnum, the dog seeming to sense his agitation. Rexell pushed open the doors and went inside. The hall was quiet, and apart from the stench of the worm slime which was overpowering, seemed normal.

"Where do we go, Mag?"

The dog growled low in its throat, then padded along the corridor, coming to a stop by a door recessed into the wall. Rexell caught up, patting the dog on the head.

"Makes sense, that's where I'd go if there was a quake." He pushed open the basement door, reeling at the intensity of the smell coming from within, and then started down the steps, curious as to what he would find. At the bottom of the staircase was another door, the glass in it cracked. Magnum started to growl, tail pushed between legs, lips curled back from teeth.

"Easy Mag, let me go take a look." The dog snorted and sat as Rexell pushed the door open. "Jesus, this is bad."

The room looked like it should have been a maintenance area, however, there was no real sign of it anymore apart from the boiler half hanging from the wall and the ruptured pipes which were spewing into the gaping hole where the floor should have been. The earth had been dug away from beneath, the entire room now hanging over a black void. The edges of the earth below, bare dirt and broken pipes, was lined with the same translucent slime as the wormhole outside. Hanging above the hole, pinned to the ceiling with the same substance, were a half dozen cocoons, the shapes enough to tell Rexell that they contained people.

"They must have come here after the worm started attacking," Rexell said as he stepped into the room, dirt falling from the thin edge of tile which remained. Magnum stayed where he was, growling at the threshold of the door, its agitation clear.

"Keep it down Mag."

Magnum whined, and fell silent, pacing in the hall outside the door. Rexell could sense it too.

They weren't alone.

He leaned over the hole, staring into the newly created void. The earth below was crisscrossed with holes, large burrows which had been created by the worm as it went about its business. As bad as the smell had been when they first entered the school, here it was even worse, almost unbearable, the ammonia-like stench making Rexell's eyes water. He crouched and touched some of the slime around the perimeter of the floor, rubbing it between his fingertips, which went numb almost immediately.

"Shit," he grumbled as he wiped his fingers on his trousers. It dawned on him that he had no idea what to do. His first plan had been to go into the burrow and maybe leave some mines down there and then draw the worm out, however, the numbing properties of the slime meant that such an idea wouldn't work. He glanced back towards Magnum, who was at the door again, growling low in his throat.

"Dammit Mag, will you just...." He turned back to the burrows, the rumble growing louder. A breeze touched his face, sending another wave of that same putrid smell towards him, and he knew it was coming.

He stood, intending to retreat back, but as he did the worm burst from below, fat and slick, and much, much quicker than he anticipated. Rexell lost his footing, slamming shoulder first into the door and almost pitching into the abyss. The giant worm was half out of its burrow, its maw open and slick as it snapped and probed the air, looking for him. He saw teeth, concentric rings gnashing and snapping. Rexell turned back towards the door, his foot slipping in the slime. He fell, chest slamming against the broken edge of the floor, legs dangling just feet from the worm. He tried to grip the doorframe, but it too was covered with slime, his hands numbing quickly. He knew he was going to fall, and that those teeth would be waiting. He tried to dig his feet into the soft earth, but it crumbled away, his useless arms flailing as he fell closer to his certain death.

Magnum lurched forward, grabbing Rexell's jacket in his jaws, feet scrabbling as he tried to pull his master to safety.

The Alsatian growled and drooled, pulling with all its strength. Rexell's backward momentum halted, and he was able to get an elbow planted on the floor, giving him the purchase he needed to pull himself higher, Magnum dragging him to the safety of the hallway. Rexell lay there panting, stroking Magnum who sat, tongue lolling beside his master.

"Come on, we need to go get some weapo-"

The floor exploded under him, launching him halfway up the staircase in a shower of dirt and concrete as the worm broke through, determined not to lose its prize. Magnum yelped and scrambled to safety, waiting for Rexell on the upper staircase as the worm once again snapped at his legs. Bloody and dirty, he blinked away the thunder in his brain, staring at the worm in dumb half recognition as it lurched towards him. He moved, diving to his left as the worm spat its translucent venom, which landed in the space he had just occupied. Rexell scrambled for the steps, the thunderous roar of broken concrete and displaced earth for company as the worm gave chase.

"Mag, go, get out of here," Rexell screamed, wiping the blood from his forehead.

The worm was almost on him, rearing up again and spraying more venom. Rexell dived for the steps, smashing into them in a graceless heap. He knew he was in trouble. The numbness that had started in his fingers had now spread to his arm. His thoughts felt slow and ponderous, the perpetual ringing in his ears making everything seem like it was taking place underwater. He didn't fear death, but at the same time wasn't quite ready to meet his maker yet. He lurched, mostly on instinct, half climbing, half crawling up the steps, Magnum just ahead and pausing every few feet to look back and check his master was following. Rexell burst out of the basement and into the hall, unsure if the deep rumble he could hear was the worm giving chase or the concussion he was sure he had received. Time seemed to slow.

The ammonia stench of the worm's venom.

The steady patter of bright red blood on polished school floors from his face. He had no idea how badly he had hurt himself but suspected it wouldn't be pretty. He ran for the door, dust clouding from his clothes as he made for the exit. He almost fell out of the door, pausing to take a breath and watch as the blood continued to patter from his head onto the floor. He stared at it as it started to vibrate, the concrete cracking beneath him. Once again, instinct took over, and he dived to his right as the worm came out of the ground, snapping at him, a high pitched whine coming from somewhere within it. It lurched for him, snagging his jacket in its jaws, which retracted into its mass, pulling him with it.

Panic.

He began to slide, pulled towards the creature's mass. He scrambled, clawing at the pavement, ignoring the pain as he ripped his fingertips against the harsh concrete. Everything became surreal, alien almost. He glanced over his shoulder, aware of the blood pounding in his temples as he was pulled towards it. The worm changed, the skin around its mouth peeling back into four distinct sections, widening its gullet so that it would easily be able to take him. He could see the slime covered teeth inside, row upon row lining these new, banana skin like sections. He could only imagine the damage it would do. His body would be pulverised, reduced to a bloody mush. There was no fighting it, the thinner tube with the concentric teeth, he now saw, was just a clasper, something with which to cling on to its prey before drawing it into the mouth proper. The muscular appendage was pale and muscular, pulsing as it pulled Rexell closer to his death. It was then, just as he had begun to accept his fate that Magnum acted. The Alsatian charged, leaping at the grasper and sinking his fangs into it, growling and shaking his head in order to try and free his master. The worm reared back, releasing its grip, which was all Rexell needed to shrug out of his jacket. Both he and Magnum broke into a shambling run as the worm retreated back into its burrow.

He could see Shaw as they approached the camp, his nose still bloody, eyes already starting to swell. Pertwee was with him, apparently in the process of trying to make some kind of peace, when they saw Rexell approach, whatever they had been talking about forgotten. He fell, landing hard on the ground, panting and trying to make the dull incessant throbbing in his brain subside. He could see them standing above him, mouths moving and speaking words which went unheard. He blinked, trying to bring them into focus. Shaw had a cocky grin on his face as he shouted at Pertwee, pausing intermittently to point at Rexell.

Cody lay there, the world too bright, the buzz in his head starting to subside. He touched a scratched hand to his forehead and stared at his claret fingertips. He stared at Shaw, who was still shouting at Pertwee, who nodded intermittently, unable to get a word in. Having said his piece, the commander retreated, disappearing back into his tent.

Pertwee turned to Rexell, the anger, even in his dazed state difficult to miss. "You've embarrassed me. Embarrassed the government. I knew you were no good. I knew it was a waste of time. Now it seems I've been proven right."

Rexell tried to get up, but his legs buckled and he fell back down. "I can do it. I need to...rethink that's all."

Pertwee shook his head. "Forget it. I was just waiting for your arrogance to trip you up and now it has."

Pertwee leaned closer, nose inches from Rexell's, teeth exposed in a sneer. "You think you were ever going to be set free? You think you were ever going to be patted on the back and left to go out into the world. Are you really that stupid?"

Rexell stared, trying to make sense of it all.

"Even if by some miracle you had been successful and stopped this thing, you were always going back to Alcatraz. You have no idea how hard it was to go along with you and your stupid arrogant ideas of what should be. You, my friend, shouldn't believe so much in your own hype. Now, we do things my way. The military way. As for you, you're going back to prison for the rest of your miserable, stinking life."

Rexell lurched to his feet and grabbed Pertwee by the shirt, almost lifting him off the floor. This time, however, Pertwee wasn't frightened. "What are you going to do? Hit me? Rough me up? It won't change anything. You're still going to rot."

He wanted to hurt Pertwee, that much was true, but he knew that would make his situation worse. He knew he shouldn't have been surprised by the betrayal by the government, and for that, he had to blame himself. To him, saving the children who were cocooned in the school was key. He saw Shaw's men, lining up behind Pertwee, soldiers with weapons poised and ready to take him down. He ignored them, glaring at Pertwee.

"I ain't done yet."

"You're finished. Look at you. You're a mess. You're not a professional. Just a street thug with a big reputation. You're scum."

"I'm not done yet," Rexell repeated, shoving Pertwee away from him and into the group of waiting soldiers.

He turned his back, ignoring the barked commands of Shaw's men who were telling him to stay where he was. He ignored them, taking his chances and walking towards the barricade.

"It's alright, let him go," Pertwee said as he straightened his jacket. "We have a tracker on him anyway."

Rexell headed towards the crowd, Pertwee's voice ringing in his ears.

"You can't escape this. We have people coming. A whole team just to take you in, dead or alive."

Rexell ignored it, trying not to give in to the anger inside him. On seeing the near seven foot, blood covered giant of a man, those behind the barricade dispersed, letting him through. He could see his car, his beloved Shelby, Marion leaning on the hood. He saw the look on her face when she saw him, repulsion perhaps, maybe a little fear. He supposed he must look like shit to be getting such reactions.

"What happened, are you alright?" she asked as he stumbled towards the car.

"Stay here, I have a job to finish," Rexell replied, pushing past her and getting into the Shelby, wiping the blood from his eyes. He looked at her from behind his crimson mask as Magnum leapt into the passenger seat through the window. "See you around, honey."

"You're leaving?"

"Not exactly in the way I wanted. I should have known not to trust an asshole like Pertwee. You take care of yourself."

"Where will you be? Where will you go?"

"Go tell Pertwee to get those kids out of the school as soon as I'm clear."

"You didn't answer me."

He smiled and started the engine, its throaty growl drowning out any potential response. She watched as he floored the accelerator, the car snaking towards the barrier. The watching crowd dispersed, moving to safety as Rexell smashed through the barricade. Pertwee and Shaw ran out of the tent, trying to flag him down as he passed heading back towards the school. He drove the Shelby towards the burrow in the street, then skidded to a stop, black tire marks left in his wake. He revved by the burrow, the engine note loud and crisp, the vibrations reaching the worm in seconds. Rexell waited, staring in his rear-view mirror at the burrow.

The worm came, lurching out of the ground. Rexell dropped the car into gear and drove away from the school, the worm diving back underground and giving chase, the tarmac pushed up from the road as it followed. Rexell maintained his speed, making sure he didn't get too far ahead of the worm. He led it out of town, and then as he reached the scrub wasteland on its edge, he went off-road, the car snaking as it struggled for grip, a rooster tail plume of dust behind it.

Still, the worm continued to give chase, its speed increasing as it moved into open country. Rexell pushed the car harder, engine screaming in his ears, Magnum sitting in the passenger seat, tongue lolling as he looked at his master. Rexell ignored it.

All he focused on was the terrain ahead and ensuring he didn't run over a rock or hit a ditch which would end their chase prematurely. Ahead, he saw what he was looking for, a stretch of flat, open land. He increased his speed, pushing the car up past ninety as he put some distance between himself and the worm. Without warning, he put the car into a spin, kicking up dirt and dust as he made a complete turn, grinning as he moved towards the approaching creature. Sensing that its prey had turned to challenge it, the worm breached, launching towards the car, opening its maw to full capacity. It was this that Rexell had been waiting for. He changed gear and accelerated towards the creature's maw, closing his eyes as it enveloped the car. He thought of Michelle and Jose as his world turned to black.

III

Shaw drove the green jeep, Pertwee in the passenger seat and staring at the tracker, homing in on its position. They had seen Rexell lead the creature away, and as instructed, had rescued all of the children from the basement of the school. Pertwee's glanced up from the screen as they jostled through the uneven countryside.

"Slow down, he's just over that rise."

Shaw grunted, keen to get his hands on Rexell and give a little payback for the broken nose. "I hope that worm didn't kill him before I get a chance to have a few words of my own."

Pertwee said nothing and turned his eyes back to the tracker. "Alright, you should be able to see him soon."

The jeep crested the rise, and both Shaw and Pertwee were shocked into silence.

The worm lay on the surface, its side split open, a huge mound of putrid organs fanned out over the sand.

"Where is he, I don't see him." Shaw snapped.

"Right there. That thing must have killed him."

"Until I see a body, I'm not assuming anything." Shaw snapped.

"Well, let's go take a look."

The two men climbed out of the jeep and approached the creature, the putrid smell making them wince as they approached. It had already started to rot under the burning hot sun. Pertwee gagged, Shaw almost threw up. They walked towards the creature, staring at it in wonder now that the threat was gone.

"Looks like it burst, its goddamn guts are all over the sand. Looks like your boy did us a favour after all before he bit the big one." Shaw said as he crouched by the huge hole in the creature's side.

"He's not dead," Pertwee muttered.

"Say what?" Shaw replied, turning towards Pertwee, who stood by the creatures head.

"I said, he's not dead."

Shaw strode towards him, brushing sand off his green trousers. "What the hell are you talking about, of course, he –" Shaw stopped speaking, staring at the small object balanced on the creatures head. "What the hell is that?"

"Tracker. It was in Rexell's arm."

"What the hell is it doing here?" Shaw snapped, already knowing the answer.

"He cut it out."

"Bullshit he did."

Pertwee wasn't listening. He stood and looked out over the valley, an endless void of desert land and scrubs. "I wouldn't underestimate him, Commander Shaw, despite your feelings towards him."

Shaw opened his mouth to respond when they heard it, the unmistakable distant growl of a supercharged Shelby GT somewhere in the distance.

"Son of a bitch," Pertwee muttered as he watched the plume of dust kicked up on the horizon.

"We'll track him. Hunt him. He won't get away." Shaw said, his cheeks flushing red again.

"Not yet you won't."

"What do you mean?"

"That's not our call. I need to call it in. Speak to the President."

"You can't just let him get away. That son of a bitch assaulted me."

Pertwee didn't respond, he watched as the plume disappeared, the engine note growing more distant. No matter what happened, be it leading a team to hunt him or letting him go as per the original agreement, he was sure that one way or another, they hadn't seen the last of Cody Rexell.

Cody Rexell will return...

Don't miss out!

Visit the website below and you can sign up to receive emails whenever Michael Bray publishes a new book. There's no charge and no obligation.

https://books2read.com/r/B-A-LSFB-RUUQ

BOOKS 2 READ

Connecting independent readers to independent writers.

Did you love *Cody Rexell: Monster Hunter*? Then you should read *Cody Rexell and the Cannibal Death Camp*[1] by Michael Bray!

Cody Rexell is back, and still doesn't give a F*ck!

His adventures this time take him to the heat of the Mexican jungle. Barely escaping with his life from a remote village of bloodthirsty cannibals, Rexel is determined to go back and retrieve an item of great importance that was taken from him.

When a face from the past betrays Rexell and threatens to send him back to the government who are still searching

---

1. https://books2read.com/u/bpWAEk

2. https://books2read.com/u/bpWAEk

for him, he reluctantly agrees to help with a covert mission to locate a drug baron who has gone missing in the jungle. As the group embark on what should be a routine mission, events unfold that puts the lives of everyone at risk and forces Rexell to revert to his uniquely violent methods to ensure those under his supervision survive.

Read more at www.michaelbrayauthor.com.

Also by Michael Bray

Cody Rexell
Cody Rexell: Monster Hunter
Cody Rexell and the Cannibal Death Camp

Hell on Earth
The Dark Place

Terror Tales
Terror Tales: Volume Two
Strange Tales
Terror Tales: Volume One

The Project Apex Trilogy
Project Apex: Book Two

Standalone
Burger Van: A horror anthology
Crawl
Something in the Dark
Funhouse
Forgotten Fears
Shoebox
Dark Corners
I Was Jack the Ripper
A Truth Stranger Than Fiction

Watch for more at www.michaelbrayauthor.com.

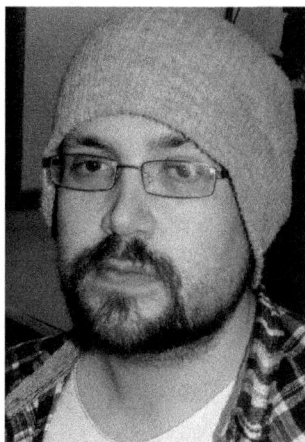

About the Author

Michael Bray is a bestselling author / screenwriter. Influenced from an early age by the suspense horror of authors such as Stephen King, Richard Laymon, Shaun Hutson, James Herbert & Brian Lumley, along with TV shows like Tales from the Crypt & The Twilight Zone, his work touches on the psychological side of horror, teasing the reader's nerves and willing them to keep turning the pages. Several of his titles are currently being translated into multiple languages and he recently sold movie rights to his novel, MEAT with production planned to take place in 2017.

A screenplay written by Bray / Shaw based on their co written novel MONSTER was picked up for distribution by Mandala Films, with both Bray and Shaw set to produce / direct the movie, taking his career into new territory as he looks to write more for both the literary world and the screen. Where to find Michael Bray online Official website: www.michaelbrayauthor.com Facebook: www.facebook.com/

michaelbrayauthor Twitter: www.twitter.com/
michaelbrayauth Instagram: www.instagram.com/
michaelbrayauthor Google +: www.plus.google.com/
michaelbrayauthor

Read more at www.michaelbrayauthor.com.

Ingram Content Group UK Ltd.
Milton Keynes UK
UKHW021838160623
423552UK00013B/333